I0604028

DIANE E. TATUM

Book 4
Main Street Mysteries:

DNA Secrets

By
Diane E. Tatum

ISBN: 978-1-0881-6530-0

Dedicated to
my romance hero husband Ken,
my sons Dan and Brad,
their wives (my true daughters) Becca and
Julie,
and my four grandsons Ethan, Kellan, Paul, and
Jonathan.

Endorsement:

Tatum's latest addition to her Main Street Mysteries series is full of her typical attention to detail and page-turning action. When Ross and Dorie can finally start their new life together, Dorie's first day on her new job opens a proverbial can of worms that sends them into a tailspin. Always delightful and thought-provoking, Tatum's work, and especially a contemporary mystery like DNA Secrets, is sure to please the Christian reader.

Lisa Lickel, author of Buried Treasure and Meow Mysteries series

"For I know the plans I have for you," declares the LORD, "plans to prosper you and not to harm you, plans to give you hope and a future." Jeremiah 29:11 NIV

Do not be yoked together with unbelievers. For what do righteousness and wickedness have in common? Or what fellowship can light have with darkness? What harmony is there between Christ and Belial? Or what does a believer have in common with an unbeliever? What agreement is there between the temple of God and idols? For we are the temple of the living God. 2 Corinthians 6:14-16a NIV

For he chose us in him before the creation of the world to be holy and blameless in his sight. In love he predestined us for adoption to sonship through Jesus Christ, in accordance with his pleasure and will— to the praise of his glorious grace, which he has freely given us in the One he loves. In him we have redemption through his blood, the forgiveness of sins, in accordance with the riches of God's grace that he lavished on us. With all wisdom and understanding, he made known to us the mystery of his will according to his good pleasure, which he purposed in Christ, to be put into effect when the times reach their fulfillment—to bring unity to all things in heaven and on earth under Christ.

In him we were also chosen, e having been predestined according to the plan of him who works out everything in conformity with the purpose of his will, in order that we, who were the first to put our hope in Christ, might be for the praise of his glory. And you also were included in Christ when you heard the message of truth, the gospel of your salvation. When you believed, you were marked in him with a seal, the promised Holy Spirit, who is a deposit guaranteeing our inheritance until the redemption of those who are God's

possession—to the praise of his glory. Ephesians 1:4-14
NIV

Books by Diane E. Tatum

Main Street Mysteries series
Book 1: *Kudzu Sculptures*
Book 2: *Gemini Conspiracy*
Book 3: *Attic Visitations*
Book 4: DNA Secrets

Colonial Dream series
Book 1: *A Time to Fight*
Book 2: *A Time to Love*
Book 3: *A Time to Choose*

Gold Earrings
Mission Mesquite
Oxford Fairy Tale
Dreaming of a Wedded Christmas
Cecilia's Y2 Key
Finding Love in the Fog of Aphasia

Chapter 1

Getting Ross and Dorie home …

Daelin Police Captain Riley McDonough stood in Atlanta Hartsfield Airport waiting for Ross and Dorie MacAvoy's flight to land from their honeymoon in Scotland. He had taken them to the airport on Christmas day following their wedding on the twenty-fourth.

"Look over here. I bet this is their flight!" Jenny Schaefer had come with him. She was staring out the window, waiting for planes to land. "Riley, come look and tell me if I'm right."

Riley sauntered over to where Jenny and her ponytail twitched with excitement. He slipped his arms around her, timidly at first then with growing confidence. They had been dating just since the wedding. A whole week, although it seemed to Riley it had been longer than that. He'd known her longer as his favorite waitress from his regular stops in the Corner Café where she waited tables. Then she turned up cooking and waiting on guests at Ross and

Dorie's wedding a week ago. They'd been dating ever since while his best friends had been in Scotland.

Now the plane was late, and they'd still have the drive to Helen after Ross and Dorie deplaned, went through luggage retrieval, Customs, and Border Control. Maybe it had not been a good idea to bring Jenny along for this prolonged experience.

"Ladies and gentlemen, American Airlines Flight 36 from Edinburgh, Scotland, is now arriving at Gate 25."

"Thank God." Riley was feeling impatient and unsure, two things he hated to feel. He'd rather be in control of a situation.

"They're here!" Jenny ran to the exit from the secure terminal area.

In some ways, she reminded him of Dorie. She was vivacious, energetic, and excited. Like Dorie, she was barely five foot tall and an athletic build. Their hair color was different. Dorie was from St. Louis, though, and from a family with her three brothers.

"It's still going to be a while before they come out. Why don't we get coffee?" Riley steered her toward a Starbucks Coffee shop. "We can get a pastry or a sandwich or something."

"Aren't you excited to see them?" Jenny walked backward while talking to Riley. "They could have cool souvenirs. And they've been married, you know, for a week."

"And that's something I will not be asking about when they arrive." Riley chuckled and steered Jenny to walking forward to avoid the oncoming crowds.

Riley's phone chimed, indicating a text message. "Ross says they are at the gate and preparing to get off the plane. He'll keep me informed."

Jenny probably didn't need a cup of coffee. She was bouncing while she walked. Would she crash on the way home, or rev up even more? Hard to tell. This relationship was still so new.

"Hurry, Riley, we don't want to miss them."

"They can't get home without us."

The line was long, but there was plenty of time. Once they ordered and received their coffee and food, Riley guided Jenny to a bistro table in the walkway.

"I've been meaning to ask where you go to church. I'd be happy to go with you or you can go with me." He took a bite of iced pound cake to give Jenny a chance to speak.

"Hmmm. Well, I really don't go to church regularly." Jenny sipped her coffee. "Is that a problem, Riley?"

Riley took a deep breath. "It depends. Are you a Christian?"

"Sure, I'm an American living in the Bible Belt." Jenny peeled the paper from the muffin she'd chosen. "My foster mom and dad didn't take me to church. After their deaths, I was adopted by my foster aunt Flo Schaefer who runs the Doll House B&B in Helen. Sunday mornings are premium for cleaning with guests coming and going."

Riley's heart sank. *Was she a believer? What were her thoughts about faith and Christ?*

Riley's phone chimed again. "They have their luggage and are headed for Customs and Border

Control." He drank a long sip of his espresso. He would talk with her about Christ. That would need to wait for a day when she was open to listen. He had a responsibility to share his faith before the relationship became too serious.

Dorie was glad to be on Georgia soil once again, but thoroughly exhausted by the nine-hour return flight. Ross had the two bags they had taken, and she rolled the new bag nearly bursting with souvenirs, gifts, and Ross's new wool suit.

They approached the official US border agent's booth together. He looked at them both and at their passports.

"You just came from Scotland?"

"Yes, sir. It was our honeymoon." Dorie had been telling nearly everyone they had met on this trip.

"Your passport is in your maiden name then?"

"Yes, sir. Is that a problem?" A glance at Ross and she knew. Flames of blush painted his throat and face.

"Do you have another form of ID with you, ma'am?"

Dorie dug in her purse and produced her driver's license.

"Where do you live now? Is either of these addresses correct?"

That's when Dorie had an inkling of fear. "No, sir. I live at Ross's house. The address on his passport."

The agent checked Ross's passport. "Get those documents updated, Mrs. MacAvoy."

"Yes, sir."

He stamped both their passports. "Welcome home to the United States of America. Congratulations on your marriage." He then grinned a toothy smile.

Ross roared with laughter. "Thank you."

Dorie's face grew hot. Ross pulled her through the aisle and into the terminal.

"He was just giving you a hard time." Ross laughed again.

Dorie dragged her luggage behind her. "How was I to know to update my passport and my license, so they at least had the same address? I didn't know we were going international for our honeymoon."

"No, you did not. That's what makes it a surprise, y'know?" Ross walked backward and gave her a smile.

Dorie stopped and sat on her bag.

Ross rolled his luggage up to her. "Let's go home to our own bed."

She crossed her arms. "I don't think I can move another step."

"Ah, Darlin', you're just being stubborn now. Come on. Riley and Jenny are waiting to drive us home." He wrapped his arms around her. "I love you."

"Okay, but I am so tired. You may end up carrying me."

A porter approached them. "Do you need help with your luggage?"

"Apparently we do." Ross picked Dorie up.

"I've got my wife. Can you get the three bags?"

The porter smiled. "Yes, sir."

People in the terminal began clapping and cheering.

Dorie threw her arms around Ross's neck. "What are you doing? You're embarrassing me."

"No, Darlin', I'm taking you home." Ross held her close. "There's Riley and Jenny."

"You can put me down, Ross." Dorie faced forward and saw Riley and, yes, Jenny from the B&B.

"Once we're out of the secure area, I'll put you down. If you want me to, I'll carry you all the way to the car. I only want what's good for you." Ross held her close then set her down on her feet. "I know you're tired. I am, too. Let's just go home."

"Welcome home!" Jenny rushed up to Dorie and threw her arms around her neck.

Ross shook Riley's hand. "Thanks for picking us up. With a date?"

Riley shrugged. "We'll see about that."

Dorie and Ross followed Riley and Jenny to the parking garage. The porter took the bags all the way to the car. Ross tipped the porter and threw the bags in the back of the car, then climbed in.

Riley started the car. "Next stop, Helen, Georgia."

Jenny and Dorie chattered all the way home. Ross dozed in the front while Riley drove.

"They get on well, don't they?" Ross muttered. "Sleeping is nigh on impossible."

"Yeah, Jenny's a live wire. You might remember her from the wedding."

Ross nodded. "Niece of Flo of the Doll House B&B?"

"That's the one." A semi passed them causing the SUV to shudder.

Ross opened one eye and looked at Riley. "You don't sound sure about her."

"It's only been a week."

"Well, I've only been married a week. I'm sure."

Riley huffed. "You only dated six months before that. How could you be sure enough to marry her?" He guided the car off the interstate at the Daelin interchange and headed up the mountain road to Helen.

Ross shrugged. "When it's the one, you know. I knew as soon as the coffee dried on my Sunday shirt and tie."

As they drove through Helen, Riley stopped at the Doll House and dropped Jenny there. He drove up to Ross's renovated farmhouse on the ridge. Once he unloaded Ross and Dorie's luggage, Riley headed back to small town Daelin, Georgia, alone.

Chapter 2
Beginning a new year …

Dorie woke wrapped in Ross's arms. She could so get used to this. So far marriage to Ross was all she ever dreamed it could be. She snuggled in for the few moments left before the alarm went off. Today was the first day of her new job at Daelin PD. The wind whistled around the eaves. The bed was warm, but the day was bound to be January cold. She turned and wrapped her arms around Ross.

"You awake, Darlin'?" Ross sounded groggy. "First day, right?"

"Yeah, first day away from you. Sleep okay?"

"Always sleep better next to you."

The alarm sounded. Dorie kissed Ross and wriggled out of his arms. Ross rolled onto his back and stretched. Dorie giggled then headed to the bathroom to get ready for work.

When Dorie got out of the shower, the smell of coffee invited her to the kitchen. She threw on her clothes for the day then hurried to join Ross in one of their favorite pastimes, drinking coffee.

"You look beautiful, Darlin'." Ross handed her

a cup, expertly prepared with her choices of cream and sugar.

"Thank you." Dorie took a sip and sighed. "You get it right every time."

"I'll work on putting away all the Christmas stuff. We still need to open all these wedding gifts some time. Tonight?" Ross sipped his coffee. Ross was waiting until spring for his forest ranger job to open up at the Chattahoochee Ranger Station on the Appalachian Trail.

Dorie enjoyed seeing her handsome, strong husband, leaning against the counter in his sweatpants, no shirt.

"Caught you looking." Ross grinned his goofy grin. "Like the view?"

"I get to look now. I'm your wife." Dorie checked the time. "Any Pop-Tarts left after my brothers were here? Time is slipping away."

Ross checked the pantry and cabinets. "Here's the unfrosted strawberry ones with a Post-it note: 'Yours, I believe. Terry.'"

"Perfect. Could you toast two while I get my shoes?"

"As you wish." He wangled his eyebrows.

"Really? *Princess Bride* references this early in the day?" Dorie threw him a kiss as she climbed the stairs.

When Dorie returned, Ross was at the bottom of the stairs. He held a Thermos of coffee, two Pop tarts wrapped in a paper towel, and her backpack with her laptop and purse. She stood on the first step so she could be eye-to-eye with him.

"You're amazing, my love." She kissed him. The kiss grew passionate. "Stop. I have to go to work."

Ross embraced her around the waist. "So now that we're married, we have no time. Is that what you're telling me?"

Dorie leaned in for another kiss. "No, just not at this time. I love you."

He laughed and held her. "Ditto, Darlin'. I'll miss you. Have a good day. No dangerous stuff, right?"

"Right." She squirmed out of his grasp and pulled on her coat. "Have a good day."

Dorie scooted out the door to their SUV before Ross could detain her further. The wind was cold and blustery. Snow flurries spit at her as she unlocked and loaded her things into their blue vehicle.

Ross was tasked with picking up Star, their retired racing greyhound, from Lilah Andrews who kept her whenever they'd be gone for a longer time.

Until this morning, Dorie had come to Daelin to be a reporter for the *Daelin Beacon*. Her experiences thus far had her wind up in the center of police investigations. That made good press, but some things she needed to know that the police department could not tell her unless she worked for the police. Captain Riley MacDonough was Ross's best friend and had become close to her as well.

Long story short, Riley had offered Dorie a job as Liaison Officer/Research/ Communications on the detective squad, and she had taken it. Ross was fearful about what things Riley would allow her to get entangled. She'd already nearly been killed in

August, been threatened by a hostile man out for revenge in October, and nearly killed in her bed and bashed in the head in December. How much worse could it get? Perhaps if she was included in police procedures, she'd know what danger might be coming her way. At least she'd have backup in these situations.

Riley had agreed that she could write as a free-lancer for her former editor Ethan Andrews at the conclusion of each case. Dorie would also interface between the police and the public – press releases, conferences, and statements. She'd still be writing, but her research would be from within the police jurisdiction. It seemed like a good fit given the history she had experienced since May. Dorie headed the car down the Daelin road from Helen on the mountain.

Riley fidgeted in the lobby of Daelin PD waiting for Dorie to arrive.

"Can I help you, Cap?" The desk sergeant came over to the door and looked out. "What's going on?"

"Dorie MacAvoy is joining us today. I wanted to welcome her." Riley checked his watch again.

Sarge checked his watch. "She's not late, Cap."

"I know." Riley jammed his hands in his pants pockets. "I'm just anxious to bring her on board, officially."

"Right, just don't forget she is Ross MacAvoy's wife now." Sarge chuckled. "Before the wedding, you might have had a chance."

Riley turned to him. "Don't need your advice, Sarge. Get back to the charge desk."

Sarge backed away, grinning. "You got it, Captain." He returned to his desk.

As Riley turned back to the door, Angela the proprietor of Java Joint was coming in.

"Hey, Riley. Is Dorie here yet? I brought her favorite mocha coffee with two extra shots for her first day on the job." Angela balanced two to-go cups in a carrier. "I also brought you your espresso, black as always."

"Thanks. She hasn't arrived yet." Riley checked his watch again.

"You look worried. She's not late yet, is she?"

"No. I just worry about that mountain road." Riley turned away from Angela. She could read just about anyone.

"That's not what you're worried about, is it?" Angela handed him his cup and looked him straight in the eye. "You still love her, don't you?"

"Ridiculous." Riley took a sip of the hot brew. "I'm just nervous. Not sure how our friendship works now."

"Dorie hasn't morphed into a siren or a banshee. She's still just Dorie. Being married shouldn't change who she is." Angela set the carrier down on a table then hugged Riley. "No worries."

He squirmed out of her embrace. "I just want to act appropriately, you know. I wouldn't want to hurt her or Ross." He took another sip. "I didn't even know I felt that way until this morning."

"Don't borrow trouble. I've got to get back to the shop. Tell her good luck." Angela left Dorie's coffee on the table in the lobby and took the carrier back to Java Joint with her.

Riley watched Angela until he saw Dorie's blue SUV pull into the lot. She stopped to speak to Angela. He picked up the coffee and dropped it off in Dorie's new office, then returned to his own office. She didn't need to know he'd been waiting for her.

"Here ya go, Dorie." Sarge directed her into Riley's office. "Our new Liaison Officer, Captain. Have a good day. Let me know if I can help."

"Thanks, Sarge." Dorie settled into the chair in front of Riley's desk. "What's on tap for today?"

"You have an appointment at ten at the Crime lab. They will do DNA swabs and finger printing and any other tests deemed necessary for our records. Once the DNA results come in, they'll do a deep background check. Just routine." Riley tapped a pen repeatedly on the desk. "You should settle into your office. Angela brought you coffee, it's on your desk. Get familiar with the computer programs we use. After lunch, you should tour the station and meet everyone."

"Pretty quiet today?" Dorie shrugged out of her winter coat.

"So far. Beginning of the year. Just some drunks drying out in the cells." Riley wiped his sweaty palms on his pants. "Guess criminals know Dorie Hudson … MacAvoy is on the case. Sorry."

"No worries. My passport and driver's license both say Hudson." Dorie grimaced. "The Customs and Border Control officer thought it quite funny, actually. So did Ross. One of my first tasks in the new year is to correct my driver's license."

Riley came around in front of the desk and sat on the edge. "You will also be getting an ID badge with your picture. It can be your first with your married name."

"Can I get my driver's license fixed too?"

She looked at him with those sweet, beautiful eyes.

"Of course, not much on today anyway. You need to be lawful to drive." He clicked the pen top too many times and then laid it on the desk.

"Aren't I the one who should be nervous, Riley?" Dorie lifted her eyebrows. "Why are you so fidgety? We're supposed to be friends."

Riley nodded, probably too much and willed himself to stop. "We are. It's just a new situation. You're married to Ross. I'm your boss."

Dorie dropped her eyes to her hands in her lap. "I still love you as a friend. You don't have to feel strange with me. You, Ross, me-Three Musketeers. I'm just changing where I hang my shingle."

Riley nodded, again too much. "I don't want it to be awkward. You know how I feel."

"I married Ross." Dorie stood. "I'll go take care of my stuff and drink some Java Joint coffee. Let me know what I can be doing to be helpful."

Chapter 3
Settling in at Daelin PD …

Dorie gathered her coat, Thermos, and backpack and headed to the office with her name stuck to the door on a Post-it Note. Sure enough, a Java Joint to-go cup sat on the desk. She hung her coat on the hook on the back of the door, unpacked her backpack, and slipped her purse into the bottom drawer of the desk.

As she turned on the desktop computer, Dorie found a Post-it Note with her username and password. She'd have to change that password immediately. She was deep into the databases and computer files when a knock on the office door startled her.

"Mrs. MacAvoy, these flowers came for you."

Dorie couldn't even see the desk sergeant for the profusion of roses, holly, and alstroemeria, a giant replica of her bridal bouquet. She directed him to a short file cabinet beside the desk. The red roses perfumed the small office. The holly recalled the holiday and the wedding. The lily-looking alstroemeria was reddish-pink. Her favorites.

"Thank you, Sarge."

Dorie plucked the card from the bouquet and

laughed when she read the sentiment. "Love, Ross. Yes, I did actually buy and send these myself." She remembered the flowers a homeless lady named Sally had sent her with Ross's credit card, at Emmie's instigation.

She spent the morning immersed in databases, information that she'd not been privy to as a journalist. After a few hours mining the gold from these sources, a screen popped up reminding of her appointment. Dorie jumped up and hurried down to the Crime Lab.

Dorie walked into the sterile environment, white and splashed in bright light. People in lab coats reminded Dorie of her recent hospital stay. Her head still felt bruised from the bat bashing Emmie gave her prior to her wedding.

"Can I help you?"

The voice brought Dorie back from her musings. She looked down at the curly, black-haired, brown-skinned woman before her at the desk.

"I'm here for my ten o'clock appointment for DNA sampling, fingerprinting, and whatever new employee tortures you must enact."

The young lady rose from her seat and stretched out a hand. Dorie grasped it.

"You must be the infamous Dorie Hudson MacAvoy. I've heard so much about you. I'm Chloe Freeman, lab tech. Come with me." She released Dorie's hand and led her over to a seat next to a counter full of paraphernalia. "I don't know what Captain McDonough has told you about the in-processing tests. You really should have done all this before your first day of work. I guess Cap didn't want to interfere with your wedding and honeymoon."

"DNA and fingerprints were all he said." Dorie scooted into the seat with a moveable arm board, which when moved across the body could be used as a restraint against the squeamish. Chloe moved the board to allow Dorie's arm to rest on it.

"We're also going to take some blood to scan for abnormalities." Chloe pulled the rubber strap tight around her arm above the elbow and thumped to find a good vein.

"Abnormalities? Like what?" Dorie's heart quickened.

"Blood count. Viruses. Cancer. Pregnancy." Chloe stuck the needle into a vein and hit pay dirt first try. Blood spurted into test tube after test tube. After five tubes were filled, Chloe took the needle out and covered the poke with cotton and gauze held in place by a stretchy strip of purple tape.

Dorie complied with Chloe's order to hold her arm up and clenched. "I don't understand. Why does the PD need all that information?"

"Well, if you are going to be in the field, you should be physically fit. Don't want any officers caring for you when they should be chasing a suspect. We'll also be doing a confirmation DNA test to match up with the cheek swab."

"I received a DNA testing kit for Christmas." Dorie fidgeted in the seat.

"Cool. But everyone in the police department has a DNA sample in the database. It's to rule out your DNA should any end up at a crime scene. Same with the fingerprints.

After Chloe swabbed her cheek, she sent Dorie to the bathroom to give a urine sample as well. Dorie left it in the little two door slot in the wall. She washed her hands and used the blower to get them dry, but in the end, she wiped her hands on her pants.

Exiting the restroom, Dorie found Chloe.

"Anything else?"

"Just one more thing, as Columbo always said. We need a chest x-ray. Could you change out of your bra? Let me know when you've accomplished that."

Chloe led her to a changing room near the X-ray machine.

Dorie went in and took off her sweater and bra and folded them together leaving her wearing a long sleeve, black t-shirt with her black jeans.

Chloe led her to the Radiology area. "Any chance you could be pregnant?"

Dorie giggled. "I guess there's a chance."

Chloe put a lead apron over Dorie's abdominal area, moved Dorie into the correct position, then took the x-rays from the safety of a booth. When the tests were done, Dorie redressed.

"I'll let you know when all the test results come in. Go up to Processing to get fingerprints done." Chloe walked with Dorie back to the entry desk.

"Thanks, Chloe. I hope we can get to know each other better."

"If you're working with the detectives, we'll see each other plenty." Chloe laughed a tinkly laugh. "Congrats on your marriage. Good luck in your new job."

"Thanks." Dorie left through the swishing automatic sliding door and headed up to Processing for fingerprints.

As Dorie was wiping the ink off her fingertips, Riley stuck his head into her office.

"We need to go. There's been an incident we need to attend."

Dorie grabbed her coat from the back of the door, snagged her purse from the drawer, and followed Riley out to the Captain's cruiser. Sirens started on the car as soon as Riley left the lot. Additional sirens joined the wail from behind them. After a short drive down Main Street, Riley pulled up to the First Baptist Church in Daelin that Dorie and Ross attended.

"What's going on?" Dorie asked as Riley tossed her a bullet proof vest from the back of the SUV.

"The alarm company for the church indicates an unauthorized entry to the building this morning. The suspect may still be in the building." Riley wrapped his own vest around himself. "No heroics, Dorie. I mean it. You are at my side, nowhere else."

"Got it." Dorie nodded and snugged her vest a little tighter. "Ready."

Pastor Greg was talking with patrolmen in front of the building when he looked up and came over to her. "Dorie, I heard you were back from your honeymoon. How's Ross treating you?"

Dorie smiled. "We're great. What's going on here?" She saw Riley roll his eyes.

"I think that's my line. You're not the press now." Riley shook his head and motioned for Pastor Greg to answer Dorie's question.

"I let the staff have today off. They work so hard

up to and over the holidays. Normally we don't have much to do in January." Pastor Greg sat down on the step. "I got a notice from the alarm company that someone had entered the building, so I called Daelin PD and just got here myself."

"Are you assuming the intruder is still inside?" The patrolman had his incident book out and was taking notes.

"I guess so, unless the sirens scared him off."

"Or her?" Dorie was also writing in her new incident book. "Have you seen this person?"

The pastor shook his head. "Like I said, I just got here too."

Riley waved two patrolmen into the front part of the building, and a second pair went with the pastor who opened an end door for them. Another pair waited at a middle door, in case the suspect tried to escape. He waved Dorie back to the car.

When the door in the middle of the church opened, the four officers came out.

"Cap, unless he's hiding somewhere, he's not here now." The officers holstered their service weapons.

Dorie breathed again. She hadn't realized she'd been holding her breath. Riley also exhaled and drew in a deep draught of air.

"Scene is clear then, Toby?" Riley put his gun away too.

"We didn't go into the rafters, the attic, or the baptistry. The office has been trashed. Hard to know what's been taken if anything."

Riley sent the pastor in with a pair of patrolmen to determine what might be missing. Another pair searched for possible clues to the identity of the thief. A third pair began a canvas of the area for surveillance film and eyewitness reports.

"What can I do to help?" Dorie put her incident pad and pen away.

"You know the building, right?" At her nod, he continued. "Go in and look through the Sunday school rooms and closets for anything that seems out of place. If you see blood or obvious fingerprints, don't touch it. Call one of the patrolmen. When the forensic team arrives, they will need to document that evidence."

Dorie nodded and headed for the building while pulling on her nitrile gloves.

"Dorie, if you come face to face with the intruder, don't try to be a hero."

"Gotcha." As she entered the building, the forensic team pulled into the parking lot.

Chapter 4
A little drop of blood …

The only thing found at the church was a trashed office and a little drop of blood at the window where the thief gained entry to the building. The forensic team collected the drop and dusted for fingerprints at the window and each of the crash bars on the exit doors.

After checking every room, Dorie returned to the church office. Pastor Greg was picking up and straightening papers. Dorie bent down and to help him with the things from the floor.

"It just doesn't make any sense, Dorie." Pastor Greg took a journal from her and placed it in order on the shelf. "Nothing seems to be missing."

Dorie handed him another volume labeled 1970. "What are these?"

"Membership rolls. At the beginning of each year, the church membership was recorded in the appropriate journal. As the year progressed, members were added and subtracted." Pastor Greg picked up another volume. "Of course, now days we keep the roll on the computer. We still print it out and stick in the front of a journal." He handed her last year's journal.

Dorie opened it. The previous year's list of members was printed and stapled into the front. She turned to what would be May and found her name, the church she attended in Blacksburg, Virginia, where her membership had been during college, and her townhouse address and cell phone number. In December, Pastor Greg had recorded Ross and her Christmas Eve wedding with her new last name and address.

Once they had placed all the journals on the shelf, it was apparent that several were missing: 1976, 1979, 1994, 1996, and 1998.

"That's odd. My birth year is 1998. Probably just a coincidence." Dorie wiped her dusty hands on her black jeans, leaving handprints.

"Dorie, I learned a long time ago that there's just no such thing. Everything happens in God's time and plan. Everything is a God-incident. He may not cause the events in our lives, but He's also never surprised by them either." Pastor Greg wiped a hand against his sweaty brow. "While each volume has no monetary value, the intrinsic value to our history as a church is priceless. Then the privacy of the information with the prevalence of identity theft is another issue. We need to find them and bring them back."

"We'll do our best, Pastor." Dorie hugged him. "If there's nothing else I can do, I better get back."

"Didn't you ride with Captain McDonough? I can give you a ride back to the station."

"Not necessary. Ross and I walked all over Edinburgh, Scotland, on our honeymoon over New

Year's week. Surely I can walk down Main Street for a few minutes." Dorie pulled on her coat and noted her purse was still in Riley's cruiser. "I'll be fine."

"If you're sure." Pastor Greg nodded. "Be safe."

In just a few minutes, Dorie was back at the Daelin PD. She found an official looking nameplate on her office door and her purse on her desk. She stashed the purse in her desk drawer and began a search on church break-ins during the last year. While the computer chugged away, Dorie ate the lunch Ross had packed for her.

The word Chloe had said jumped unbidden into her brain in regard to the blood and urine tests. *Pregnant?* While they weren't taking particular action to avoid pregnancy through mutual agreement, the idea of her becoming pregnant in the first two weeks of their marriage was, well, frightening. Not disagreeable, just unexpected. What would Ross say? She shook her head. She knew he'd be delighted. That's why they'd decided not to use birth control.

When Dorie and Ross had discussed it, Ross had said, "If the Lord wants to give us a child or ten children, we should accept them all. God has a plan for each of them. I was an only child with no parents most of my childhood. I wish I had the brothers you have. A child, today or years from today, is a welcome gift from God. Do you think differently?"

Dorie found herself in tears, but they were not sad tears. She felt the same way as she had on that day. "One doesn't reject a gift from God, do they?" had been her reply. She wiped her tears. "Blessed be the name of the Lord." Faith was putting feet to what you say you believe.

Riley stuck his head in her office. "Hey, you busy? I'd like to meet with the detectives about the break-in."

"Sure." Dorie cleared her throat. "Let me print off this info about church break-ins in the area. Where are we headed? Can I bring coffee?"

"Conference room just past the break room. Yes, to coffee." Riley gave her an odd look. "Have you been crying? What's wrong?"

"Nothing's wrong. I just realized that I've made a commitment that seems more likely now than before." Dorie clicked the print button and paper began spitting from the printer.

"I don't understand." Riley leaned against the door jamb. "Don't you like it here? Are you missing your job at the *Beacon*?"

Dorie laughed. "Nothing like that." She grabbed the paper, her laptop, a pen, her phone, and her Thermos. "I'm ready."

Riley divested her of the laptop and printout. "Do you need a cart for a meeting?"

"Do you want me to get the facts correct when I talk to the public?"

"Definitely. We'll get you a laptop to use in the conference room, so you're not using your personal laptop at work. It will be more secure that way." Riley backed out of the doorway. "After you, Mrs. MacAvoy."

Once the detectives joined Riley and Dorie in the conference room, theories about the crime were bantered about, dismissed, or added to a list of possible purposes.

"There must be something specific the thief is looking for at the church. The years of the journals are specific. They didn't take a decade of journals. The gap in the years is specific as well. The intruder was looking for specific information." Detective Matthew Akers doodled on his notepad. "Could it be a search for a mother and child?"

Dorie typed in his idea and the years. "If the mother was born in 1976, then the other journals would be a search for the child or children. They would be my age."

Detective Jordan Mavers set down his coffee mug. "That rules out the mother. She knows where and when she was born. So that might make the child the suspect, y'know, trying to find his or her birthmother."

"Foster system, adoption records. I noticed we have an extensive database from the state." Dorie made a note to check those years. "Is it possible that the thief never intended to take the journals, but instead was disturbed by the alarm system?"

Detective Akers nodded. "Yeah, he or she only meant to access the journals but gathered them up to escape the police or pastor showing up on site."

"Nothing else was taken? No money or artifacts?" Mavers sipped his coffee.

"Artifacts? In a Baptist church?" Dorie laughed. "You must not be Baptist. The closest Baptists get to artifacts is the picture of Jesus with long wavy hair praying in the Garden of Gethsemane in brown sepia tones with holy light from heaven descending. It's in, like, every older adult Sunday school classroom across the convention, Detective Mavers."

Mavers raised an eyebrow. "Call me Jordy. Catholic. So, Baptists don't have old relics or precious metal or gemstone encrusted crosses?"

"If we did, and it's a pretty big if, they would be stored in a safe deposit box or a safe." Dorie waved her pen at him. "If the church had such a thing, the thief wouldn't be stealing journals. They chronicle people, not treasures."

"Good point, Jordy. Newbie got you on that one." Detective Akers gave Dorie an in the air point for her remark. "Call me Matt. We need to track a search for a biological mother and/or a family member."

"I can start on that." Dorie made a note in her incident book. "I'll also check these church break-ins."

"I'll ride the lab about getting back DNA on the blood drop. It's the only hard evidence we've got." Matt noted his self-assignment. "Jordy, get patrol's report on anyone who might have seen the suspect enter or leave the church."

"What about the family tree websites that you can get DNA to prove your lineage? Once we get lab work back, the DNA might lead us to family members." Dorie laughed. "My younger brother got us all those DNA test kits for Christmas. I told him he was crazy because we'd all have the same DNA, am I right?"

"Might rule out extracurricular parenting." Jordy snorted.

"Not in her family." Riley finally spoke up. "I

think we're done here for now. Get busy. Let's get the church's journals back."

The detectives gathered their note sheets and meandered back to their office. The clock showed four o'clock.

"Go home, Dorie. I'm sure Ross has had a frustrating day without you. You can start on the paper chase tomorrow." Riley put his hand on her shoulder. "It's great having you here. You're every bit as good at detecting as Mavers and Akers. I think they were surprised."

Dorie laughed. "See you tomorrow then." She ducked out from under his hand and headed toward her office with her arms full of her note-taking technology.

Chapter 5
New beginnings …

"Ross! I'm home!" Dorie struggled in the door with her belongings and plopped them by the door. "Something smells great. What are you cooking?"

She found him engrossed in stirring a pot of chili, earbuds in each ear and singing along. Dorie came from behind him and slipped her arms around his waist. The spoon in his hand went flying across the kitchen, splattering chili as it went.

Ross ripped his earbuds out. "Dorie!" He grabbed hold of her. "I didn't hear you come in."

"Clearly." Dorie slipped his embrace and picked up a dishcloth to wipe down the walls and floor. "Guess I'll never do that again."

"Ah, Darlin'." Ross raised her from the crouch she was in. "Welcome home."

They kissed and hugged.

"That's more like what I expected." Dorie reached for the spoon in the corner of the counter.

"How was your day? Eventful?" Ross washed the spoon and laid it on the stove top in the spoon rest.

"They're running a pregnancy test." Dorie watched for his reaction.

"What? You shouldn't be standing here then." Ross picked her up and carried her to the living room. "Are you?"

Dorie shook her head. "Not that I know about. It gave me pause though."

"I bet it did." Ross kissed her as he set her on the couch. Then he sat down beside her. "Why are they doing a pregnancy test?"

"Chloe said it was to know if I was suited for field work. I don't expect to be chasing any criminals though." Dorie snuggled into his chest. "We agreed to be surprised, remember?"

"That would be a surprise, for sure." Ross burrowed his head into her hair. "I had a surprise today as well. The National Forest Service called."

"Really?" Dorie sat up and looked him in the face. "What did they want?"

"I start work tomorrow in the Chattahoochee Forest. One of the guys on the winter rotation fell down a hillside and broke his ankle. He's out for the rest of the season, so they hired me now instead of in the spring."

A splash and a hiss summoned Ross and Dorie to the kitchen in a flash. Ross grabbed the handles, then stopped and grabbed for potholders. He pulled the pot from the burner while Dorie rinsed out the dishcloth and carefully wiped around the burner.

"I guess dinner's ready." Ross proclaimed with a sheepish look. "Think there's a Crockpot in one of those wedding gifts we haven't opened yet?"

Dorie nodded. "That would probably be a good

thing. We should open more of them tonight since we're home."

They both laughed.

Dorie and Ross completed chores around the house, getting everything ready for the night and for both of them going to work the next day.

"When are you on?" Dorie called from the kitchen to Ross who was bringing in Star.

"Three days and two nights. Then home three nights and two days."

Dorie walked out to the living room where Ross tussled with the Star, their greyhound.

"I missed you so much, Star." Ross rubbed his head and chest and wrestled with her.

"That will make for a couple of lonely nights. What will you eat?" Dorie rubbed in the hand lotion she'd applied after washing dishes. "Can you call out? Should you take an Alexa Show so we can talk at night?"

Ross stood, wiped his hands on his jeans, and came to her. "Don't worry. I'll stop at the grocery on my way into the ranger station. There's a stove, refrigerator, pots, and dishes. Each ranger will have a shelf for his own food. I won't starve. There's a bunk room to sleep in. Someone just has to be on site in case of an emergency."

She wrapped her arms around him. "What kind of emergency?"

"A hiker in distress. A wild animal problem. A forest fire." Ross wrapped his arms around her. "Don't worry. I've trained for all these events. The ranger station is not that far from here."

"We've had our share of emergencies, too." Dorie hugged him tighter. "How do I get a hold of you?" Tears overflowed despite her will to control them.

"Come on, let's head for bed." Ross turned off the lights and followed her toward their upstairs bedroom. When they reached the cherry sleigh bed, she laid down on it, and he climbed in next to her. Star rattled her crate as she also bedded down.

Ross kissed her. "You're not alone, Dorie. Star's here with you. Melody is just down the road." He kissed her again. "Angie and Riley are just twenty minutes or so away in Daelin." Ross turned off the lamp beside the bed. "And I'll be home three of five nights, here with you."

Dorie whispered in his ear. "Then I guess it will be okay, Sweetheart. Follow your dream."

"I am. The ranger job can wait until the morning."

Dorie made it downstairs before Ross on Tuesday. She smiled when she saw Ross enter the kitchen in his forest ranger uniform. "Wow, you look amazing."

Ross blushed. "A man in uniform. I get it."

"Then you don't understand me at all. I love you whether you're in uniform or not. You are a handsome man, sweetheart." Dorie handed him a cup of his favorite brew. "You're my ginger-haired giant of a man."

"Ah, Darlin'." He sipped the hot coffee, set down his cup, and reached for her. "I love you, too. You make me not want to leave you for my dream job."

"I'll be here when you come back. Pop-tart?" Dorie stretched on her toes and kissed him. "Have a great three days. Get food on the way."

Ross sipped his coffee and ate the unfrosted strawberry pastry. Dorie sipped her coffee and leaned against him. He wrapped an arm around her. She savored their remaining moments together.

Ross dropped by the mini-mart on the edge of the Chattahoochee Forest and picked up essentials: coffee, half-n-half, hamburgers, buns, cheese slices, lunch meat, bread, and sandwich spread. A bag of chips and one of salad greens rounded out his purchase. He'd have to figure out what he'd need on the fly.

He parked his truck next to a small gray truck and carried his purchases and duffel bag inside. No one seemed to be around, so he put his duffel on the unused bed and stashed his purchases on an empty shelf in the fridge. A Keurig coffeemaker sat on the counter. Perfect. He'd brought his reusable cup just in case.

Ross headed into the office and sat down at the lonely-looking desk. As he booted the computer, he looked around for a status sheet. It would tell him which hikers were on the Trail nearby, who had checked in, who might need help.

The door slammed in back of the station. Ross looked up and headed toward the sound.

The ranger took off the green uniform jacket and

hung it next to Ross's. Then she flung a curling long strawberry blonde ponytail out from her collar. When she turned, she startled.

"Oh my! You surprised me." She clutched her uniform shirt. "I'm Felicity Johnson. You must be Ross. Welcome." She stretched out her hand.

Ross shook her hand. "Ross MacAvoy. I'm replacing William Parton."

"Glad to have you here. Luckily, it's been quiet. Just a reported bear sighting near the Trail. I went over to the site, but I didn't see anything unusual."

"Good. I don't want to wrestle a bear on my first day." Ross laughed. "Maybe on day two."

Felicity laughed. "It's a good thing to wait on."

A hello from the front office sent the two of them scrambling.

"Hi, how can we help you?" Felicity got to the hiker first. "What's going on?"

"I wanted to see if there's a package from home here. Mom was supposed to send me some new boots." The tall hiker wrapped his arms around himself. "Heat, it's a good thing. Can I warm up and charge my cell phone while I'm here?"

"Of course. What's your name?" Felicity took his ID and headed back to the storage room where packages were stored for hikers on the Appalachian Trail.

Ross showed him a charging station and encouraged him to rest while his phone charged. Felicity brought a package out to him.

"Here you go, Jake. Boots from Mom. I bet there are treats too." Felicity smiled and handed him the box and his ID back.

"Thanks, guys. I think I'll sleep for a few. Is that okay?"

"Absolutely." Ross nodded and took a seat at his desk. "Are you in the system, Jake?"

"I registered before I started." Jake stretched out on the couch next to the charging station.

"Perfect." Ross looked him up in the database and marked him at the Chattahoochee Ranger Station. "It will make your mom glad to know you've checked in."

Jake nodded and immediately fell into a hard sleep.

"I wonder how long since he slept well." Felicity sat in the desk chair across from Ross. "What questions do you have?"

"My wife wants to know if I can have an Alexa here to talk with her." Ross rocked in his chair. "We're newlyweds."

Felicity nodded. "She's insecure about you being here. Wait until she finds out your partner is a woman. I can feel her jealousy from here."

"Wait. Dorie is very secure." Ross could feel the blood course into his face. "Besides, you assume I'm attracted to you. I don't even know you."

"True, but we'll be sleeping in the same room tonight." Felicity jumped up and headed for the kitchen.

Now that would torque Dorie. I'll leave that part out. Ross shot a text to Dorie. "Got here safe. Already have a hiker here. New partner is a woman."

Chapter 6
Looking for a needle …

When Dorie read the text, the words stunned. *A woman? Why would he tell me such a thing?* She would already miss him tonight. She didn't need to also feel in competition with someone she didn't even know.

The knock on the door startled her back to her surroundings.

"Dorie, can I bother you?" Chloe entered the office. "I come with test results."

"Do I get to keep my job?" Dorie waved her over to her side chair. "Sit. Talk. I can use the company just now."

"Everything looks fine. You don't appear to be pregnant, though if it's recent it could still be a false negative, if that's what you're concerned about." Chloe took her hand. "Even if you were, your job doesn't require physical exertion."

Dorie exhaled a breath she didn't know she was holding. "It's not that I don't want to have a child. I just don't know that I'm ready to have one now."

"Well, girl, it would be nine months from now, technically." Chloe grinned. "No worries, it turns out. What are you doing for lunch? Want to share a space? We could walk down to Java Joint."

Dorie grinned. "I love Java Joint. As long as I'm here, I'm in."

"Great." Chloe smiled. "Eleven, okay?"

Dorie nodded. Maybe Angela wasn't her only friend now.

When Chloe left, Dorie turned her attention back to the list of church burglaries she was researching. Most incidents were like the one at First Baptist: nothing missing of value, records rifled. *What is someone looking for?*

Jordy stuck his head in the doorway. "Hey, Dorie, any clues in your research?"

"Just that someone is looking for somebody's information. Any info from the blood drop?"

"Not yet. It will be about another day or two before the Atlanta lab sends us DNA info. Even then, the DNA has to be in the system. This suspect may have not been a criminal before now." He sat down next to her. "I wish we had the ability to test for DNA here. It would allow us to respond more quickly."

"Did we get any fingerprints?"

Jordy shook his head. "The fingerprints we found aren't in the database. Sadly, that may mean the DNA isn't either."

"That won't help much then." Dorie leaned back in her chair. "How do we find him or her?"

He stood and shoved his hands in his pockets. "We wait for another break-in. And hope for more information. So far, it's just an annoyance." He headed out, leaving her to datamine the databases.

Dorie's desk phone rang. "Hello?"

"Eleven. Lunch?" Chloe's voice.

"Absolutely."

Chloe and Dorie walked across the block to Java Joint through a flurry of snow. The wind was cold and strong. It blew Dorie's coat open, creating a strong shiver in her. They breezed into Java Joint.

"Mocha espresso and café latte!" Angela called out. "Chicken salad croissant?"

"Yes, please. Got any soup as well?" Dorie headed for her usual booth.

Chloe spoke up. "I'll take that soup too."

"Gotcha both."

"You have your name on a booth at Java Joint?" Chloe threw her coat into the booth. "You must drink a lot of coffee."

"You have no idea." Dorie put her gloves in her coat pockets. "Between Ross and me, coffee is like IV fluid."

"She ain't lying, Chloe. How did you guys meet up?" Angela placed two cups of coffee on the table.

"Chloe's at the Crime Lab. We met my first day yesterday." Dorie held the cup to warm her hands. "She drew blood and other fluids and did a chest X-ray."

"You're both good people. You should be good friends. I'll go get the soup and croissants." Angela whipped around and headed back to the coffee bar.

When Dorie arrived back at PD, Riley was on his way out the door.

"Come on. We got another church break-in."

Dorie followed him to the cruiser. Lights

flashing and sirens blaring, they drove a short distance to the Daelin Methodist Church. The pastor met them in the parking lot.

"Thank God you're here. I didn't know what to do. During our regular lunch break, our secretary Sheila was eating at her desk, and a woman came into our office and hit her in the head." The older man wrung his hands, clearly distraught. "I'm sorry. I'm Michael Nolan." He shook hands with Riley and then Dorie. Dorie made notes in her incident pad. "What did she take?"

"Nothing as far as I can ascertain." He wavered and gasped for breath. "I need to sit down." He collapsed onto the concrete steps.

The ambulance arrived on the scene, clearly to treat Sheila, but Riley waved them over to Pastor Nolan. Dorie ran across the parking lot to where Sheila was waiting to be assessed.

"I'm Dorie Hud…MacAvoy. How are you feeling? We'll get help for you as quickly as we can, but the pastor just collapsed over there."

"Oh, no! He has a heart condition!" Sheila jumped to her feet, held her head, and wept. "Let me go to him. Call his wife."

"Stay here and be calm. Let the EMTs do their job." Dorie helped her back in the office chair she'd been wheeled out of the building in. Dorie took off her coat and wrapped it around Sheila. "Just relax. Did you see the person who hurt you?"

"Not really. She was somewhat short and had a light-colored ponytail. I don't remember much else."

A second ambulance arrived and drove to where Dorie and Sheila waited. EMTs jumped from the vehicle and hurried to Sheila's side with gear to treat her.

"Hey, Dorie. You're usually the one we're taking into the hospital. What gives? You living on the quiet side?"

Dorie recognized him as the EMT who was often on duty during her too frequent incidents as a reporter. Wrong place, wrong time, sometimes as a target. "Hey, Marcus. Not me this time. This is Sheila, church secretary."

He laughed as he took Sheila's blood pressure. "It's pretty high, Sheila. We should take you in to the hospital."

"This gash in your head needs stitches, too." Dorie recognized the other EMT as Theo, also a frequent visitor to Dorie's incidents.

The first ambulance screamed out of the parking lot with the pastor. "Sheila, go on to the hospital and get your head taken care of. If you need anything or remember anything, call me." Dorie pulled out one of her cards from the *Beacon* and scribbled her new number at Daelin PD on the back. "Anything you think of, let me know."

Theo and Marcus helped Sheila into the ambulance. Soon it followed the first one out of the parking lot to Daelin Medical Center.

Dorie followed Patrolman Joel into the church office and looked around. The computer screen held the membership roll of the congregation. *Again with the records. What is this girl looking for?*

"Here's the weapon." The patrolman held up a heavy bookend with his gloved hand. "Maybe we got prints this time."

Dorie nodded. Without more information, how would they ever know what this series of break-ins was about?

Chapter 7
Twisted DNA results …

With Ross at the ranger station at night, Dorie barely slept. At five AM, her phone rang.

"Are you awake?" Ross's voice soothed her raw edges. "Dorie, are you okay?"Sis. I can sleep on the couch. That's what I did last night. It's not very comfortable."

"Sorry. I'm just a little lonely and didn't sleep last night. You should sleep in the bunk." Dorie ran her free hand through her tangled hair. "What's she like, your partner?"

"Auburn hair, from St. Louis, a journalist." Ross whispered his response. "Oh, you mean the other ranger here."

"Of course, I did." Dorie whispered back.

"Felicity is her name. You're the one I love though."

"I know." Dorie felt herself blush. "I didn't mean to imply anything. I just miss you."

Dorie sighed. She climbed out of bed and took Star down the stairs.

"Darlin', it's hard to be here without you. My first day was great, though."

"I'm glad. We've had a string of burglaries at churches." Dorie started the coffee machine. "I need to get ready for work, dear."

"I love you. I'll call you later."

Dorie pushed into her office, arms full as always. Every corner of the room was rose- scented from the bouquet Ross had sent on her first day of work. She turned on the computer. The printer did its waking up cycle, clicking and clacking and whirring, while she settled her things into their places.

A tap at her door roused her attention from the screen.

"Chloe! Come in. What do you know?"

"I know the lab in Atlanta done screwed up the DNA tests." Chloe flopped into the chair beside Dorie's desk. "Your DNA was a familial match for our intruder."

"That makes no sense. All of my family is in St. Louis."

"Exactly. They must have cross-contaminated the samples. And both of the samples came back positive for pregnancy." Chloe threw her hands in the air. "So much work wasted."

"Did you tell Riley?"

"Yeah. That's why I'm here, to drag you back downstairs." Chloe leaned in. "Then coffee break at Java Joint?"

"Sounds good."

After additional blood work and coffee, Dorie returned to her office.

"How did your blood get mixed up with our

suspect's?" Riley barged in and stood against the door. "I'm not convinced. How do you have a family member here breaking into churches? Why don't your brothers look like you?"

"What are you saying?" Dorie stood up to him, her five feet against his six-foot frame. "I don't understand."

"At the wedding, I noticed you don't look like any of your brothers or your parents. All the work we sent in Monday, you are in the middle of it all. What are the odds?" Riley placed his hand on her shoulder. "What is happening here?"

"I don't have an answer." Dorie felt herself shudder. "Are you saying my family isn't my family. How could that be? You think I'm adopted."

"I don't know, but I don't think the lab made a mistake. We'll go ahead and resubmit your blood from today." He patted her shoulder. "I'm sorry. This is much deeper than we know. You should talk to your mom. You're old enough to know the truth if you're adopted." He left her and walked down the hall to his office.

Dorie closed the door and sat at her desk. She stared blindly at her computer screen. Tears leaked from her eyes. *Was she not really a member of her own family?*

Call me! Dorie texted Ross. *My DNA matches someone in Daelin who is breaking into churches. How can that be?*

Her phone rang almost immediately. Their wedding photo showed on the screen.

"Ross, what's happening?" She wiped the tears from her face. "How can I be related to a woman in

Daelin?"

"It's okay, Darlin'. You're still you no matter what your DNA says." He paused. "I love you no matter what."

"I know. But did my family lie to me all these years? Am I not a Hudson after all?"

"Dorie, what's the worst thing that could be true?" Ross chuckled sarcastically. "My mother murdered my father, grandparents, and died alone in a prison mental hospital."

"Am I adopted? Do I have a sister?" Dorie spoke in hushed tones. It was not so bad compared to what Ross had experienced.

"Who is looking for you, I gather."

"But she hurt someone yesterday and caused another to have a heart attack. How good can she be? And I'm related to her?" Dorie grabbed a tissue from the box on the shelf to wipe the cascade of tears from her face.

"Darlin', relax. You are who you are no matter whose DNA you share. I love you and only you. Besides, you're a MacAvoy now."

"I know. I love you, too." Hearing Ross's voice soothed her nerves. "Thank you for knowing what to say. The lab is re-running my blood work."

"I'll be home tonight. Hang in there until then."

Dorie heard a female voice in the background, Felicity no doubt. "How's it working out with your partner?" She tried hard to keep the sarcasm out of her voice.

"It's fine. I'll be glad to be home and sleep in my own bed." Ross sounded tired. "Sleeping in a bunkbed in the ranger station is not one of the perks."

"I guess I should get back to work. I miss you, Ross."

"I'll see you tonight."

He hung up sooner than Dorie had hoped, but he'd calmed her. And really the lab work had probably just been cross-contaminated. She plowed into the foster care database. Thousands of children who experienced being a ward of the state. A needle in a stack of needles.

"Dorie!" Riley called out before he opened her office door. "We've got another case."

She clicked the database closed and picked up her necessaries to go to another crime scene.

"Where are we headed?" Dorie climbed into the cruiser and strapped on her seat belt.

"Hit and run with a child on a bicycle." Riley kept his eyes on the road. "It's not pretty, so prepare yourself."

"Is he/she dead?" Dorie gulped. *Guess this is where the road gets gritty.*

"He wasn't when I got the call, but he's probably not going to make it." Riley pulled up to an intersection covered in glass and blood. The bike lay mangled on the side of the road. The ambulance pulled out as Riley came to a stop. "Do you need to stay in the car?"

"No, I'll be fine." Dorie took out her incident book and a pen to take her notes on the scene. Seeing the amount of blood on the street nearly made her sick.

"What do we know, people?" Riley took charge as soon as he got out of the vehicle.

"Todd Wilkins, 13, riding his bike. He came to

the intersection, stopped at the corner according to witnesses, the car swerved 'like on purpose', hit him, and drove away." The patrolman shrugged. "Ambulance guy doesn't think the kid will be alive when they reach the Medical Center."

"What do we know about the driver?" Riley barked. "Did anyone see the driver or notice the car?"

"Red compact. Woman driver with a light brown ponytail. Didn't get the plate, Cap."

Riley swore under his breath. "Dorie, when we get back, I need you to write up two press releases. One about the church break-ins, and one about this accident."

Dorie nodded and returned to the car. She bit her lip as she looked at the tangled remains of the bicycle. Who would do such a thing? Why wasn't she paying better attention? Why did a young boy have to die? Light brown ponytail?

"Riley, a light brown ponytail?"

"I heard. It does not mean it's …" Riley turned away.

Chapter 8
Hudson family tree …

Dorie arrived home about five, but Ross wasn't home yet. Maybe she'd cook something, after she checked her email. She booted up her personal laptop and headed upstairs to change into sweats. She let Star out of her crate and into the back yard.

Star bounded across the yard with abandon, sliding on ice in some places. Dorie laughed at her. Star shot past her back into the warmth of the house. Dorie wrangled Star into the sweater her mom had knitted for her. Her mom. Was she even her mom? She shook her head and headed back to the couch and her laptop. Her latest email was from her brother Terry.

Dorie,

Here are my DNA results from that family tree site. No real surprises. Says the Hudsons are from, guess where, the Netherlands. It also says we have German and French ancestry, also some Scandinavian. Guess that's where Aaron gets his sugar white hair. Doesn't explain your auburn hair, though I've heard it's just an

American trait from the amalgamation of nations here. I may start tracing the family tree. I guess you haven't had time to send yours in yet, with the wedding, the honeymoon, and starting a new job. Slow down, enjoy your life. Happiness to you, Sis.

Love, Terry

Terence Hudson was a legal aid lawyer who helped people who wouldn't have been able to afford decent counsel without legal aid. Like all her brothers, he was tall, six-foot four inches. He also had brown hair and brown eyes, like her, except he didn't have the red highlights. He'd bought the house next to Mom and Dad, so he could be there if they needed him. Terry was a good man and always protective of his baby sister.

Sis? What if he wasn't her brother? Maybe she was the red-headed stepchild people talk about.

The front door burst open and with it, a blast of frigid mountain air.

"Honey, I'm home!" Ross, of course.

Dorie slid the laptop onto the couch and jumped up and ran to him. Star got to him first, jumping and curling around him with her long tail whipping the door, the hall tree, and Ross. By the time he'd closed the door, Dorie was at his side, too, with arms around his waist. Several bear hugs and deep kisses later, they moved to the couch. He plopped down into the spot she'd just vacated, next to the laptop, and pulled her into his lap.

"I've always wanted to say that." His scratchy beard nuzzled into her neck. "It makes me happy to know you'll be home when I get here." He kissed her ear. "I missed you so much."

Star barked at them.

"Me too." She hugged him tighter. "How are things in the woods?"

"A few hikers checking in and getting mail. A bear sighting near the trail. Stupid paperwork on all of it." Ross sighed. "In the spring, I'll have more to do than sit at a desk."

"And Felicity?" Dorie pulled away from him, so she could stare him straight in his blue eyes. "Truth?"

Ross fished in his pocket for his cellphone and pulled up a picture of him and Felicity.

Dorie saw a petite athletically built woman. Her long blonde ponytail had red highlights and curled at the end, reaching her midback. Ross had his hands in his pockets but wore her favorite smile for the camera.

"Don't be jealous. She's not my type." Ross put on his little boy look. "Truth."

Dorie gave him her best look of "utter not buying that." "Seriously, except for her hair and a bit more muscle, this could be me."

"Ah, my lass. Therein is where you are wrong. What's on the outside is merely wrapping. What's inside is what counts to me."

Dorie's insides turned upside down. "You're sure?"

Ross hugged her to him. "You are the only woman I love. You are the only one with whom I want to spend the rest of my life."

Star jumped up next to Ross and broke up the snuggling. Dorie headed for the kitchen to fix dinner while Ross took Star out for another romp in the backyard.

As Dorie got ready for bed, Ross climbed in. "So, what's the deal with the blood work?"

"Don't know. It probably was just cross contaminated with our suspect." Dorie finished in the bathroom, turned out the light, and headed to the bed.

"Does that happen often?"

Dorie climbed into their bed. "Riley says no. What does that say? What if my bloodwork is correct?"

"But you're not pregnant?"

Dorie kissed him. "No, unless it's a false negative."

"It's okay. I was just getting used to the idea." Ross hugged her close. "No worries. When God knows we're ready, He'll send us our bundle of joy."

"I'm sure you're right." She snuggled in next to him.

"Turn off the lamp, Dorie. And come on back over here to me."

She turned off the lamp on the nightstand.

Chapter 9
Following up …

Dorie enjoyed a breakfast cooked by Ross, since he was off for the next two days, before she headed to Daelin. She was a little early, so Dorie stopped in at Java Joint.

When she stepped into the shop, the bell tinkled.

"Dorie, dear friend! How I have missed you!" Angela rushed around the end of the coffee bar and grabbed her. "I haven't seen much of you since the wedding."

Dorie hugged her tightly. "I'm not as free to come and go in this new job. I was early, so I stopped by."

"I'm so glad you did! Mocha double shot espresso, on the way. Sit, sit, sit. I'll bring it to you."

Dorie headed to her signature booth and scooted in. Before she even removed her coat and scarf, Angela had joined her with a croissant and a coffee. Dorie opened her purse.

"No, no. Today is on me." Angela scooted into the booth. "I only have a minute before the morning rush. How was Scotland?"

Dorie took a deep sip of her favorite coffee.

"Wonderful, cold, bright, and cheerful." Then she smiled. "It was great."

Angela smiled back. "You love him so much. He loves you too. I'm so happy for you both."

Dorie's smile hurt her cheeks. "I am so happy. I'm still trying to figure out the new job, but home is amazing. Ross is working in the Chattahoochee Forest Station."

"Wow! Things are exciting." The clanging of the bell made Angela jump. "Later, girlfriend. Let me know when Ross is away, and we could have a sleepover at your house." She hugged Dorie and ran off to serve her next customer.

Dorie grinned. She finished her coffee and croissant before heading to Daelin PD.

Riley stewed in his office. It was harder to work with Dorie involved in every case. As much as he tried to make Jenny into that person he could love, he wasn't convinced. On top of that was the doubt. The light brown ponytail in the red compact that had killed a young boy. Could it be Jenny? Surely not. What if she was related to Dorie? A whole 'nother can of worms.

A rap at his office door brought him back to reality land.

"Yes? Come in."

Jenny poked her head in around the door. "Are you available?"

Riley smiled and waved her in. She scooted in and perched in one of his chairs in front of his desk.

That pert light brown ponytail …

"How are you? I haven't seen you at the café." Jenny stuck her hands in her pockets. "I thought I'd pop in and see if you're available for lunch later."

"Lunch is iffy around here for me. What about dinner?"

Jenny's smile wattage shrank. "Working, like usual." She got up, swirling the base of her coat. "Are you still interested in me?"

"Of course, Jenny. Why would you think otherwise?" Riley got up and sat on the edge of the front of his desk. He reached out for her and held her around her waist. "It's just … busy."

"It didn't seem so busy before Dorie got home … from her honeymoon. She's Ross's wife, Riley. I shouldn't have to compete with a married woman."

Riley scrunched his nose and gave her a quick kiss. "You're not competing with anyone, Jen. Work's just busy." *Really, that's your story, Riley?* He slipped her hands from her pockets and held them. She had a bandage wrapped around her hand. "What happened?"

"Knives. I was cutting a sandwich, and the knife slipped." Jenny stepped closer to him. "If you come to the café, maybe I can take my break after I get your order."

"Sounds like a plan. I'll see you later." Riley knew his internal lie meter was screaming. Was Jenny lying about the cut on her hand? Was he lying about his feelings for her? Was she was their suspect for the church break-ins and the hit and run?

Jenny gave him a sweet kiss then turned away. She was gone in a heartbeat. He heard Jenny call out to Dorie. Dorie answered back. Were they indeed sisters?

Dorie called the hospital. "This is Dorie Hud,,,MacAvoy, Liaison Officer at Daelin PD. How is the boy, Todd Wilkins, from the accident yesterday?"

"He's in ICU. It's not good, Mrs. MacAvoy." The nurse on the other end hesitated. "I can't tell you more. His parents are here. They would have to give consent. I couldn't begin to ask them to do that now."

"I understand, ma'am. Do you think it would help if I came and spoke to them in person?"

"I couldn't say." Bells and beeps went off in the background. "I need to go now."

Dorie pulled on her coat and headed to Riley's office. "I'm going to the medical center. Todd Wilkins is still in ICU. I'm going to talk to his family."

Riley waved to her and nodded while he was on the phone.

When she arrived, the Wilkins family was gathered in the corner of the waiting room. Dorie joined the group.

"Excuse me, I'm Dorie Hud…MacAvoy. I'm the Liaison Officer for Daelin PD. How is your boy doing?"

Mrs. Wilkins wiped her eyes and sniffled. "He's not doing great, Miss Dorie."

"I'm so sorry. I saw the scene after the accident. I can't imagine your grief." Dorie took her hand.

"What are the doctors saying?"

Mrs. Wilkins began weeping again. Mr. Wilkins steered Dorie away from the group.

"Miss Dorie, the doctors are not encouraging. They do not expect him to survive." He dropped into a chair and waved Dorie to an adjacent one. "Do you know who did this to our boy?"

Dorie shook her head. "The detectives are actively pursuing leads."

"It doesn't matter. If he dies, nothing will make a difference."

"What can I do to help you? I've prepared a news release. Would you like to review it?" Dorie handed the paper copy to him.

Tears leaked from the corner of Todd's father's eyes as he read the copy. He nodded and returned it to her.

"Is that a fair representation of what happened?" Dorie handed a box of tissue to him. "Do I have your permission to send this to news outlets?"

He nodded and wiped his eyes and nose. "Yes, ma'am. It's good." He reached for his wallet and removed a picture of Todd. "Can you use this photo?"

"Yes, sir. I'll get it back to you." Dorie slid the picture into her purse.

Beeps and *bells* began going off. The family hurried to the ICU windows. Dorie began to pray. *Lord, be with Todd and his family. If it's your will, save his life. If it's not in your will to save his life, comfort this family during the struggle. Amen.* She grabbed a tissue as well and stood by to see what would happen.

The doctor emerged from the ICU. The family huddled around him to hear what he said in hushed tones. Dorie knew what had happened by the body language responses to his news. Todd's mom collapsed, weeping. His father helped her up into a chair. He folded into the chair beside her. The rest of the family cried out in grief.

Dorie walked over to the father and knelt beside him. "What's the news, Mr. Wilkins?"

He shook his head and began to weep. Dorie checked the clock and noted the time and date on the paper copy.

"I'm so sorry for your loss." Dorie knew the words were meaningless, but at least it was something. Their suspect was guilty of murder now.

Chapter 10
Mysteries and suspicions …

Dorie finished writing the press releases for the burglaries and Todd's death. She sent an email to Riley for his approval. A quick reply said, "Great work. Send it." She forwarded them to her previous boss, Ethan Andrews, the editor at the *Daelin Beacon*.

She stared at the computer screen the rest of the afternoon trying to make heads or tails of all the information on it. Dorie found a list of burglaries in Cleveland, GA, and in Athens, GA, as well. All of them involved church records. It appeared it was Daelin's turn to be victimized in this woman's search for her family.

The foster care database overwhelmed Dorie. It was a rat's nest of everything you'd ever want to know with no discernible way to find it.

Dorie decided to switch tactics and spent the rest of the afternoon searching the database for a red car registration or rental belonging to a young woman. She also sent out an APB to auto repair shops in the area to look for a red car with damage and possible blood trace. Todd Wilkins deserved justice.

Riley stepped into the Corner Café at six o'clock. It was later than some days but earlier than most. Jenny met him at the door, and they embraced as the jingle of sleigh bells welcomed him.

"I wasn't sure you'd come." They walked to Riley's usual table. She handed him a menu. In a louder voice, she asked what he'd have.

"What do you suggest?" His question was provocative, even though ordinary enough.

Jenny leaned down and whispered in his ear. "A different restaurant with us there if only I didn't have to work here."

Riley laughed. "Okay, roast beef it is. All the fixin's. A cup of dark coffee."

"You got it. I'll bring your coffee right to you." Jenny swirled around and her ponytail danced. Her bandaged hand hung at her side as she called out his order to the kitchen.

Riley's gut told him Jenny was involved in the break-ins and possibly the car incident. Was she also related somehow to Dorie? So many questions with so few answers.

"Here ya go. Coffee, dark and black." Jenny set the cup down with her injured hand and sloshed some on the table. "Sorry. I've been clumsy all day. This darn bandage makes it nigh on impossible to do my job. I'll go get a cloth to wipe it up."

When she returned, Riley took her injured hand with care into his own. "Tell me what really happened."

Jenny perched on the opposite bench from him. "I told you. I cut it with a knife while making a sandwich. Don't you believe me?" Her glare challenged him to respond.

"Sure, I believe you. I just wondered if you'd cut it on some window glass."

"I have no idea what you're talking about." She pulled back her hand and crossed her arms. "What are you accusing me of?"

The cook called out Riley's order from the kitchen. Jenny jumped up and hurried to get his plate. She returned with two plates of food, and another woman carried a glass of sweet tea to the table for Jenny.

"Riley, this is Harriet, my boss. She owns the Corner Café."

Harriet was a fifty-something heavyset woman. "I also own all the headaches. Don't know what I'd do without Jenny. You take as long as you need for your break. We're clearly not very busy tonight." She patted Jenny's arm then went to the coffee pot and made the rounds for the regulars who were there.

"Nice of her to give you the time." Riley captured her hand. "Don't be annoyed with me. I got a case to solve that involves a young woman with a light brown ponytail."

Jenny pulled back her hand. "And so I'm a suspect because I have a light brown ponytail? Riley, really?"

Riley took her hand again. "'Course not. I'm just processing the evidence. She cut her hand on broken window glass and left a drop of blood."

Jenny's features softened. "So that's why you

wondered about my hand?"

"Forgive me?" Riley held her bandaged hand as well when she stretched it out to him.

"Sure. It's okay. You are the Chief of Police here in Daelin. Only natural you'd be 'processing' clues. I cut my hand using a knife."

"Got it. May I pray over the food?" Riley wasn't sure what reaction he'd get from her over public prayer.

"As long as I don't have to pray as well." Jenny wore a quizzical look. "I don't have much experience with that. I remember some prayers from my childhood. Not too appropriate here."

Riley nodded. "It's okay. I'll do it. Lord, bless this food and our conversation. In Jesus' name, Amen."

Jenny took her hands back in order to unwrap the silverware and dig into her plate of the special pot roast.

When the meal was over, Jenny went back to work. Riley took Jenny's glass with a paper napkin and wrapped it in the paper placemat. Then he slipped it inside his jacket and zipped it up.

"Heading out, Jenny." He laid a tip on the table for her.

Jenny hurried over to him and stood on her tiptoes to kiss him. He kissed her with growing urgency. He cut the kiss short before it overwhelmed them both.

"Something wrong?" Jenny backed away a step.

"No, it's just me." Riley stuck his hands in his pockets. "I'm cautious about relationships. I want to be sure before we get too serious."

Jenny nodded. "Sure, that makes sense. I'm feeling pretty sure about you though." She gave him a light kiss. "Have a good evening."

Riley gave her a brief hug, then he paid the cashier.

The door jangled as he left. He wished he could just let go and enjoy the time they had together. *Just too many variables to consider.* Then he got in his cruiser and took the glass to Daelin Crime Lab for fingerprint and DNA analysis.

Chapter 11
Evidence by night ...

Dorie sat up in the bed in the middle of the night.

"What is it?" Ross's groggy question held more questions within it.

"An idea about the church break-ins." She threw back the covers and jumped out of bed onto the cold floor. "I need to go check on something. Go back to sleep. You go in to work in the morning."

Ross tossed the covers back over Dorie's side and rolled over. "Probably in an hour or two. It's already morning."

Dorie laughed and pulled on her robe. Then she scurried down the stairs to her laptop on the coffee table in front of the couch. Star followed her, curled and turned, then settled beside her. Dorie petted her velvety head and ears while the computer booted.

Once it had WI-FI, Dorie searched for Daelin Baptist. Once on their site, she logged in like every member of the church could. She searched until she found "Membership Rolls."

"I knew it!" She startled the greyhound with her shout. Star growled at her, expressing her displeasure, then settled again. "Sorry, Star."

Starting in 1995, every member was listed by the dates that they joined the church family. She found what could be her name and birth record with her birthdate: Dorene Annalise Mackenzie. No way was she going back to sleep now. This discovery had wide-ranging implications. First, who else had been named Dorene Annalise? Second, her parents were not her parents. Third, the suspect is probably a sister. A sister! She had always wanted a sister.

"What did you find?" Ross had descended the stairs without her notice. His presence beside her made her jump. Star barked at his surprising entrance.

"I thought you were asleep." Dorie leaned over and kissed him. "I didn't intend to make you wake so early."

"If you are finding out something about yourself, don't you think I should be part of it?" Ross placed his arm around her. "What have you learned?"

"I may be Scot as well if this is correct."

Ross leaned in to view the screen. "How do you know you are the same Dorene Annalise as this person?"

"Well, I don't. But how likely is there another Dorene Annalise born on January 15, 1998? How could it not be me? According to this church birth record, my mother's name is Selene Mackenzie." Dorie laid back into Ross's arms. "And the family I always thought was my family are not."

Ross held her tightly. "No matter to me, Darlin'. You are mine regardless. I am your family now, my love."

Dorie arrived at the police station early to check some databases for more information. She checked the adoption records. Dorie clicked on a tab labeled adoptions and put in her birthdate, January 15, 1998. In a long list of children, she finally found it. Her name Dorene Annalise Mackenzie, adopted by Richard and Helen Hudson on January 30, 2000. She was two. Terry should have remembered her coming into their family. Why had he never told her? She called him.

"Terry? I hope I didn't wake you. I forget still that I'm in a different time zone." Dorie tried to keep her feeling of betrayal out of her voice.

"It's okay, Sis. I am almost up anyway. What's on your mind so early?" Sleep edged his words.

Dorie hesitated. "Why did you decide to give everyone a DNA kit this Christmas? Did you have an ulterior motive?"

"What? I don't know what you mean. Maybe it's because it's early, Sis, but it sounds as though something has gone awry."

"I haven't received my results, but events have caused me to question your motives." Dorie felt the tears prickle the back of her eyes. "You have always been my big brother who cared and loved me. But today, I discovered that I do not have a brother at all."

"What? I don't think I heard you correctly. What happened?" Terry sounded flustered with a tinge of irate. "I am your brother, no matter what, Dorie. Whatever has happened does not change our relationship, whether by blood or law."

"So, you do know what I'm talking about after

all." Dorie felt a tear slide down her cheek. She grabbed a tissue. "Why did no one tell me I was adopted? You were old enough to know. So was Aaron, I suppose. Did no one think I should know I was not a Hudson by birth?"

The silence on the phone line made Dorie think he may have hung up.

"Dorie, the day you came into our home was the day we all fell in love with you. You were never anyone other than our dear sister." He paused, and a sob escaped through the connection. "In all honesty, I forgot you weren't literally kin. That would have been cruel to prove it to you with sheer science. Mom explained what I had done after the wedding. I am so sorry. What was I thinking?"

Dorie stood and locked the office door. No one needed to see her with tears streaming down her face. She was afraid to even speak.

"Dorie, please forgive me. I never would have caused you so much pain. How did you find out?"

A knock at the door interrupted the call.

"Are you in, Dorie?" It was Riley. "We have the bloodwork back from Atlanta."

"I'll be right there. Your office?"

"Are you okay?" Without a response, Riley continued. "Yes, my office."

"I've got to go meet with Riley. I still have questions, Terry." Dorie wiped her face, and most of her makeup, off. "Don't say anything to Mom and Dad. I'll talk to them later."

"I love you, Dorie. I've loved you from the moment you entered our house."

"I love you, too, Terry. Bye."

Dorie hung up before Terry could say any more.
So, it was true. She was adopted.
What did that even mean?

Chapter 12
Blood tests results …

Dorie rapped at Riley's office door.

"Come!"

She opened the door and sat down while he finished his phone call. The document rested in her lap. So much of what she knew about her life was built on one enormous lie. How could she reconcile that?

Riley broke into her thoughts. "The blood work came back."

"Do tell. What does the bloodwork show?"

Riley waved the paper around, then after a significant pause, he read it to her. "The blood from the crime scene and your sample do share a familial match. You are not pregnant, but our intruder is. How 'bout that?"

"That's what made her begin searching for family." Dorie gazed down at the paper in her lap. "I've discovered that I am not a Hudson by birth. That's why I am short and have auburn highlights. I'm actually a Mackenzie."

Riley jumped up from his seat, came alongside her, and kneeled. "Are you okay?"

"Working on that, sir." Dorie turned away from him. "I'm actually quite devastated."

Riley stood and perched on the edge of his desk. "Could you be related to Jenny? Jenny was a foster child who was adopted by her foster parents. Her Aunt Flo is the sister of her foster mom."

Dorie stood. "I don't know. I need to do more research to establish relationship with them or whoever else it might be."

"I got Jenny's fingerprints on her glass last night. They do not match our intruder." Riley paused. "I also got her DNA, but I don't feel proud of doing this behind her back."

Dorie nodded. "Good. I guess that means the intruder is my unknown sister. I'll start digging. Now that I know the family name, I should be able to find more information."

She stood with her notes. Riley handed her the bloodwork info. They hugged.

"You have a great family. Nothing has changed except the knowledge of the adoption."

Dorie shook her head. "Everything has changed, Riley. Don't you see? I'm not who I thought I was. I'm someone else who was blended into a different family. A gosling among the ducks."

"It will be okay. They love you, and you love them."

Dorie nodded. "I'll let you know what I find."

Ross headed into the Chattahoochee Forest. The cold created freezing fog along the way. The roads were slick in spots and desolate. He hoped Dorie had arrived safely in Daelin. In truth, he worried more about her peace of mind given what she'd discovered that morning. Family meant so much to her. How would this secret affect her relationships with them?

He pulled up to the ranger station next to Felicity's hatchback.

He called out to her as he entered the station. "Hey, it's Ross. How are you today?"

Ross walked through to the kitchen with his three days of rations. Felicity was nowhere to be found. He checked the magnetized chalkboard labeled 'Where are you?' Felicity's marker was in the Office slot. Ross moved his marker from Home to Office.

He walked to the bunkroom with his duffle bag. Felicity's things were on her bunk. The door to the bathroom was closed.

"Felicity? I'm here. You okay?"

The sounds in the bathroom did not sound okay. Ross rapped on the door.

"How can I help? Can I get you something? Soda? Crackers?"

"A prescription in my bag for nausea."

Ross grabbed her bag and searched for the brown plastic bottle. When he found it, he took it to the bathroom. "Got it."

The door creaked open. Ross placed the bottle in her hand.

"I'll see you out there in just a few minutes."

"Okay. Call if I can do anything else." Ross gave her privacy and went out to man the office.

Ross logged in to his computer to see if any

hikers were due to check in at the ranger station. He needed to check the weather station out on the deck. And he really needed a cup of coffee. He headed for his mug and Thermos in the kitchen.

Felicity staggered into the kitchen and grabbed a Coke from the fridge.

"You look rough. Did you party too hard last night?" Ross meant it to be a joke, but the stare from Felicity meant it fell flat. "Do you need to go home? It's pretty quiet during the winter. I can handle it."

"You want to know why I'm so sick?" Felicity's eyes warned him he was on thin ice with her this morning. "Morning sickness. I refuse to allow this child to obstruct the performance of my duties."

"Congratulations!" Ross wasn't sure if that was the right sentiment. "Dorie and I are looking forward to having a child."

Her expression softened. "Thanks. I didn't mean to bite your head off. Yes, I want my child. For such a tiny little being, he/she is causing me a lot of grief. That's why the doc prescribed something for nausea."

"Got it. Sorry you're feeling bad." Ross poured his coffee into his mug. "When's the due date?"

"Beginning of September." Felicity sat at the small kitchen table, popped open the soda, and took a sip. "The party was the beginning of December when we had the big snow."

Ross felt the blush coming into his face. *Way too much information!* "Gotcha." He escaped to the office just as one of the expected hikers entered.

"'Morning. Welcome to the Chattahoochee Ranger Station. Can I help?" Ross set his coffee on his desk, then stuck out a hand for a shake.

"I'm just checking in before I head out. John Carlton. Man, it's cold out there. The freezing fog was challenging." He took off his gloves. "Can I warm up a bit before I move on?"

"Sure. Can I get you hot chocolate or coffee?" Ross sipped from his own mug.

"Coffee would be amazing. And a bathroom?"

Ross pointed him to the public restroom and went back to the kitchen to pour John a cup of coffee from the urn they kept full. Felicity had disappeared, probably to the bunk room.

"Here's a cup, John." Ross delivered the hot drink to the hiker.

"Thanks. I may hold it a while to thaw my hands."

Ross nodded and went back to his desk. Felicity slid into the room and sat at her desk.

"Better?" Ross whispered across the room.

Felicity nodded. "I'll go out on the trail a little later to check on hikers and wildlife."

"I can do that. There's no need to go out."

She hushed back. "Let me do this while I can. I'll not shirk my duties now."

Ross ducked his head to view the schedules for the time he was going to be there. No way was he doing battle with "Mama Bear" Felicity.

Chapter 13
Finding family …

Dorie did a search by the last name of Mackenzie and found four. Besides Dorene and her mother Selene, Dorie found two other daughters, Jennifer Irene and Felicity Maxene.

Dorie saw Riley pass her office. "Riley!"

He swung back to her door "What's up?"

"According to the records, I have two sisters, Jennifer and Felicity. Ross's partner at the Chattahoochee Station is named Felicity, and she looks similar to me. I don't know if she is the Felicity of this clan."

"And a Jennifer?" Riley came in and sat beside her desk. "Could it be Jenny?"

Dorie shrugged. "Nothing's definite, but it gives me some starter info. I'll pass this to Jordy and Matt." Dorie leaned back in her desk chair. "Our mother's name was Selene. I was two when the Hudsons adopted me. The question I have is, what happened when I was one to cause the three of us to become wards of the state?"

Riley nodded. "That would be key to this problem. Are you okay?"

"Not really. I'm trying not to think about it." Dorie swiveled the chair. "I tell myself that I am the same person I was when I was married and came home from Scotland. But how can I be? The way I think about myself is changing."

"You know you are loved. By your adoptive family. By Ross." Riley laid a hand on her shoulder. "By me. You know how I feel."

"I do, but I married Ross." Dorie pulled away from him.

"I know. That's not what I'm trying to say though." Riley withdrew his hand. "I'm only trying to say you are not alone."

"That's become quite apparent given that I have two sisters, a mother, and a father I do not remember." Dorie stood. "I'll take this info over to the detectives."

Riley stood. "I'm sorry. I don't mean to make you uncomfortable."

"I can't work here if the reason I'm here is to 'share me' during work hours with Ross." Dorie picked up the paperwork she'd accumulated. "Ross and I agreed to this new job in the understanding that you would keep me safe from the dangers of police work. We also need you to protect me from your advances. We must be friends alone."

"We are friends, Dorie. I love you, and I know you are Ross's wife." Riley hung his head. "Forgive me. I did not mean to imply anything inappropriate."

"Okay, but I don't want to continue to repeat myself. I care about you."

Riley backed into the hall, allowing Dorie to escape.

Dorie took her information to Detective Division.

"Miss Dorie, whatcha got for us?" Jordy stood when she entered the room. "We are stone cold short of leads on both the church break-ins and the hit-and-run."

Matt pulled up a chair for Dorie. "Have you found something, Junior Detective?"

"I think so. It turns out the break-in was perpetrated by someone related to me." Emotions began welling up inside her. Tears prickled behind her eyes.

Jordy jumped up and retrieved a box of tissues. "Hey, it's okay. Take your time. We'll do what needs to be done."

Dorie took a deep breath and exhaled slowly. *Why am I so emotional?* She took a tissue, just in case.

"It turns out I am adopted, and the DNA profile shows the suspect is my sister." She sat on her shaking hands. "I found the membership rolls online for First Baptist. I'm pretty sure it's what she's looking for." She handed Matt the printed roll sheet with her name and her mother's name.

Dorie continued. "Here are the foster care records I found this morning." Her throat choked up. Her voice was gone, so she handed the paper to Jordy.

"This is great sleuthing, Dorie." Matt laid a hand on her shoulder. "I'm sorry it's so personal and difficult."

"Yeah, good work. We'll take it from here."

Jordy patted her on her back.

Dorie called Ross on her way back to her office. After a few rings, he picked up. The line crackled. "Ross, are you there"

"Barely, I'm out on the trail. We got notice of a dead bear cub. Okay if I call back later?"

"Sure."

"Love you, Darlin'."

Then he was gone.

Ross hiked the Appalachian Trail until he came upon a furry body in the path. He leaned down and turned the animal over. It was a year-old bear cub. How it escaped its den and mother was unfathomable. More unbelievable was that the cub was not yet dead. Ross took a leather gloved hand and performed light chest compressions.

"Come on, baby bear. You need to get back home to Mama."

The bear finally took a deep breath and then yawned.

"There you go. Now where is your winter home?"

Suddenly the cub righted itself and began to bawl for its Mama. Mama bear responded with a threatening growl. The cub ran toward Mama bear who stood on her hind legs near the path and growled at Ross. The cold breeze blew past them. Ross stood still to avoid provoking her.

On the breeze, the cub called his mother back to the den. Ross waited. She grunted at him, then she followed the call of the cub.

Ross exhaled. Tangling with an angry bear was not on his lists of chores for the day. Another stiff breeze carried snow past him, filtering through the bare tree limbs. He inhaled the fresh cold air. This job was his ideal. He turned and headed back to the station.

When he entered the station, Felicity called out to him. "I was about to head out to find you. What happened?"

Ross unwrapped his scarf and pulled off his gloves and coat. "Gave CPR to a one-year-old bear and faced down Mama bear. All's well."

"Your wife called. She said you didn't answer your cell phone. I told her you'd gone out to get a bear." She smiled. "Not sure that made her feel better."

"Probably not." Ross hung up his outerwear and sat at his desk across from Felicity. "I better call her back."

Chapter 14
History unwound …

When Dorie's phone rang, she was walking into the offices of the *Daelin Beacon* where she had worked as a journalist for seven months. She checked the screen. While glad to see he'd called her back, it wasn't a good time for her to talk. She declined the call and stuffed the phone into her backpack.

"Dorie Hudson, no, Dorie MacAvoy! How are you?" Alex, the city desk writer, jumped up and hugged her. "I have missed you. Are you coming back?"

"No, I need to use the microfiche dinosaur."

Greg, the photojournalist for the *Beacon*, popped his head out of his office. "Dorie! You've been a stranger. About time you visited!" He fought Alex off to get his own hug. "I miss you so much." His whisper tickled her ear.

Ethan Andrews joined the welcoming party. "About time, girl." He waited until Greg let go of her to get his own hug. After all, they lived in the hug your neck South.

"Can I use the microfiche? I need to find some

history."

Ethan smiled. "We are all about history here. Be my guest."

Once the staff had all had a chance to welcome her, even Marie the gossip columnist, she retreated to the corner of the archives and woke up the sleeping, impertinent microfiche machine. After shedding her winter clothing and grabbing a pen and notepad, she searched the drawers for a roll of film chronicling 1998 through 2000.

Dorie settled in for the hours long search for something regarding the four Mackenzie girls: Selene, Felicity, Jennifer, and Dorene,

An hour into the search, Dorie had found nothing and was only at the end of 1998. The use of the Internet search engines, like Google, had dulled her ability to sit and sift through all the information in all the papers, even a three-day-a-week small town rag. She emerged from archival 'cave,' as they called it, to find sustenance. Coffee, for sure, and an unhealthy snack.

Greg followed her to the break room. "Find anything?"

"Not yet. Microfiche is so slow and takes a toll on your eyes as well as your body. At this rate, I'll be here most of the day." Dorie stretched as she viewed the selection in the small vending machine. "Yes! Mounds candy bars! We never had those while I was here."

"New supplier as of the first of the year. But they took out my Skittles." Greg handed her a handful of change. "My stash for snacks. My treat."

Dorie plunked in the appropriate quarters and

retrieved the candy. Greg poured her coffee into the dark red campsite Virginia Tech mug she'd left behind.

"Wow! I wondered what happened to this."

"I kept it safe for you. It's so great to have you back in the office." Greg leaned on the wall beside her. "How's married life? Ross treating you well?"

"Everything's great, except for the time he's in the Chattahoochee forest ranger-ing. He's gone three days and the two nights in between." Dorie bit into the dark chocolate, coconut-y goodness of the candy. "Not only that, his partner is … a woman." She'd almost said 'my sister', but that hadn't been confirmed yet.

"He spends four nights out of eight bunking with another woman!" Greg's face turned red. "That seems highly wrong."

Dorie sat down at the table nearest them. "I trust him, but the temptation is surely there. Ross says it's not an issue. I guess I just have to believe it's okay."

Greg dropped into a chair nearest her. "How many people are actually on the Appalachian Trail during the winter? I'm surprised they'd need two rangers anyway."

Dorie sipped her coffee. "Just as bad as I remember."

"It ain't Java Joint, for sure."

"Two rangers are required because one could get hurt and need the other's assistance. Ross is taking the place of a guy who broke his ankle in a fall." Dorie finished the first half of the candy and sipped the coffee. "But Ross is happy, spending his days in the forest. I better get back at it." She stood with her mug and remaining Mounds bar.

Greg stood and took her arm. "Listen, if you need anyone, you can call on me."

"Thanks."

Greg released her. "I care about you, Dorie. Don't forget."

"I won't." Dorie escaped the break room. She liked Greg a lot, as a friend, but she seemed to get a different vibe from him today.

She sequestered herself in the cave for the remainder of the day until she finally found what she was looking for.

Dorie read it aloud. "SUV crash kills mother of three girls on the mountain road. Selene Mackenzie's Ford Explorer careened down the chasm, coming to a stop when the SUV hit a tree. Her three daughters, Felicity, 5 years, Jennifer, 3 years, and Dorene, 1 year, who were secured in the back child seats, sustained minor injuries. Their father passed away from cancer last year, leaving the girls as orphans. With no other family available, Child Protective Services has stepped in to protect the daughters. Obituary on page 16A."

Dorie printed the screen, then advanced the film to 16A. She found a picture of Selene Mackenzie, with the succinct obit. "Widow of Paul Mackenzie, mother of Felicity Maxene, Jennifer Irene, and Dorene Annalise. Member of First Baptist Church, Daelin. Burial at Oaklawn Cemetery." She printed that screen as well.

Dorie found herself unexpectedly crying. For a mother she'd never know. For three little girls taken into foster care. For a family destroyed by death and hardship. For the need to find her sisters.

Dorie also realized that her mom had initially been against her move to Daelin. Now she knew why. She also understood some of the remarks the older members of First Baptist had made in the first visits to the church.

"You look so much like your dear mother, God rest her soul."

"I'm so glad you found your way back home."

"Your mother and father were such dear souls."

Dorie had shaken them off as addled dears and that she had reminded them of someone else. She'd smiled and said something polite. She had no way of knowing they had information she could have known as early as when she first moved to Daelin last May.

Chapter 15
Looking for sisters …

Dorie gathered all her things in preparation to head back to the Police Department. When she exited the archival cave, Ethan Andrews, editor, called out to her.

"Find what you were looking for?"

Dorie gave him a thumbs up.

"We get the exclusive when it's available."

She grinned. "Always."

The staff all yelled good-bye as she left the office. Maybe she should have stayed at the *Beacon*. She hadn't realized she had so many friends there.

Dorie pulled into the Java Joint parking lot on her way back. Her candy and coffee lunch was rebelling. She wouldn't have to stay long.

"Mocha double shot! Chicken salad croissant?" Angela called out to Dorie as she entered the friendly space.

"Yes, please." Dorie felt at home here. She entered her named booth and collapsed. She hadn't realized just how tired she was after bending over that hot, ancient machine.

Angela brought the coffee and the croissant. Then she slid into the booth. "It's technically after the lunch rush and prior to the going home rush. I might have a few minutes. What's up with you?"

Dorie pulled the microfiche copies out of her notepad. "Guess who's adopted."

"No, that can't be right." Angela took the pages and read the article and the obituary. "You're kidding, right?"

"Wish I could say I was. The church break-in suspect is a female related to me. The same person who killed that child in the hit and run. This week has gone from bad to worse." Dorie sipped her coffee. "And Ross's partner at the Chattahoochee Ranger Station is a woman named Felicity."

"No!"

Everyone in the place looked their way.

Angela lowered her voice. "You would have grown up here if it hadn't been for that accident. What are the odds you'd end up working in your hometown without knowing it?"

"My mom had reacted badly to the idea of me working here initially. I had no idea that my family wasn't my biological family. I admit, it has me baffled. I had no idea I was adopted. Had no reason to think it, much less end up here of all the places in the world." She ate the curl off the croissant. "God works in mysterious ways. Guess this is one of them."

Angela reached for Dorie's hand. "Dorie, you never mind all that. You are still you. Your memories with your Hudson family are all still valid. They love you no matter what."

Dorie's phone rang. She checked the screen and declined the call.

"Mom. I can't deal with all the drama coming from St. Louis now that I know what all of them knew. Someone should have told me." She washed the chicken salad down with coffee. "It's set me adrift, I'm afraid."

The bell on the door jangled as a customer arrived.

"Gotta go. Want to come over later?" Angela jumped up and waved at the patron.

"Nah. I'm exhausted, and you work way too late." Dorie gave her the cost of her lunch and stood with her to give a hug. "Pray for me and Ross. This is so unexpected."

"You got it." Angela whisked away.

Dorie felt in her bag for her mug. She'd remembered it this time.

She drove the short distance to Daelin PD and parked in her newly labeled parking space. "Dorie MacAvoy, Liaison Officer" was the label on the sign. She climbed out of her blue SUV and carted everything into the building.

Dorie dumped her bag in her office, placing her mug on the shelf above her computer. Then she took the printed microfiche to the copier. She copied it twice then scanned it and sent it to her computer. Dorie headed over to the Detective Division.

"Hey, guys! I got something for you." Dorie called out to Jordy and Matt. She handed each of them a copy. "Here's the background I found at the *Beacon's* offices."

"This is someplace to start. Why don't you call

it a day? The weather's deteriorating. You've done your crime-fighting thing for the day." Jordy waved the paper at her. "Go home, Dorie."

"You don't have to tell me twice." Dorie went back to her office and collected her things.

Riley poked his head in her office. "Leaving? Where you been all day?"

"At the *Beacon*'s microfiche machine getting background on the Mackenzie sisters. Just got back and gave the guys what I found." Dorie stretched and shrugged her aching shoulders. "They said I'd accomplished my crime-fighting for the day."

"Be careful on the mountain road. They're saying in dispatch that there's some black ice up there."

Dorie's mind's eye saw a Ford Explorer with three little girls going over the side of the road. "I'll be careful. See you tomorrow." She picked up her backpack and headed out.

Along the mountain road, people were pulled on the shoulder left and right. Police cars with lights flashing were angled around an accident. A towing and recovery truck with flashing lights and beeping backup warnings backed to the edge of the road. At marker 20, a car dangled over a precipice, making Dorie's stomach flip.

Where did her birth mom's accident happen? She'd check when she got home.

Her phone rang through her car's Bluetooth.

"Hello?" Dorie kept her eyes on the road.

"Darlin', it's me." Ross, of course. "Are you driving?"

"Yes, and there are accidents everywhere. I

should probably call you back from home."

"As soon as you're there, call me. I love you."

Dorie hesitated. "I love you too. I'll call as soon as I can. I'll need to get Star out when I get there, you know."

"'Course. Talk to you then." Ross hung up.

Dorie felt alone in the car, zigging and zagging around the emergency vehicles. To think that she had been in a car like one of these at the age of one that had skidded over the edge … it defied understanding and made her feel sick.

When she finally arrived home, Dorie pulled the vehicle into the garage since the rain had turned to sleet. She grabbed her bag and entered the warm house. Star barked a greeting.

"I'm coming, girl." Dorie dropped her bag on the couch and hung her coat on the hall tree. She stuffed her gloves in the pockets and wound the wool tartan scarf she'd bought in Scotland around the collar.

After getting Star out and quickly back in, she stared in the refrigerator for dinner. It looked like leftover pizza was on the menu. She brewed a cup of coffee and returned to the couch and her phone. While the pizza warmed in the oven, she called Ross.

"Hi, sweetheart. I'm home." Dorie tried to sound upbeat, but the emotional day had left her exhausted. "What's new in the forest?"

"I saved a bear cub and stood nearly toe to toe with his mama bear. What's new with you, Darlin'?" Ross sounded, well, excited and happy. He never sounded so happy when he ran the garden nursery in

Daelin.

"So, I found out my birth name was Dorene Annalise Mackenzie. I have two sisters named Jennifer and Felicity. My birth mom died after going off the side of the mountain road. Her name was Selene."

"Really? What about your birth dad? Is he still living?"

"According to Selene's obituary, she was widowed. His name was Paul." Dorie sipped her coffee and waited to hear Ross's take on the situation.

"How many women are named Felicity? Could your sisters be Riley's Jenny and my ranger partner Felicity?"

"I've wondered that myself today. I don't have any proof other than the DNA in that blood drop at First Baptist. Riley got Jenny's fingerprints last night, but they don't match the intruder. He's also running her DNA." Dorie paused. She could hear Felicity in the background. "How are things with your partner?"

"Fine. Don't worry. You're the only Mackenzie sister for me."

"If she's even my sister Felicity."

The timer went off on the oven. Dorie hurried in to rescue the pizza. "I guess I should go. I've got that leftover pizza for dinner."

"I love you, Darlin'. I know this has all been a shock. Hang in and find the truth, like you always do. Call me to say good night later, okay?"

Dorie plated the hot pizza. "You got it. I love you too. And I miss you mightily."

"Same here. Bye."

With a click, he was gone back to his dream job. Dorie still felt lost. At least she had coffee, pizza, a warm house, and a faithful greyhound to lay on the floor beside her as the sleet peppered the windows and coated the trees with ice.

Chapter 16
Winter wonderland …

Ross woke on the couch in the office to Felicity shaking him.

"Wake up, Ross. I need your help." She was in her night clothes and robe.

"What's going on?" Ross struggled to shake the sleep from his mind.

"The ice storm has brought down a tree just outside. I can't believe you slept through it."

Ross sat up and stretched. This couch put a crick in his back. He needed a new plan for sleeping at the station. He'd check storage later for a cot or something. His old futon was sounding like heaven now.

Felicity stood at the window. He joined her there.

"Oh, no!" The tree in question had landed on both their vehicles. The road and forest had turned into an icy fairyland. And neither of them was going anywhere any time soon.

Felicity put her hand on his arm. "What are we

going to do?"

This side of Felicity he had not experienced. She literally shook. And reminded him so much in that moment of Dorie, home alone in this ice storm. He checked his watch. Three a.m.

"Not much to do. The damage is done. We can wait until morning to work on the tree. The real question is how our hikers are doing in this weather." Ross pulled on his ranger shirt and tucked it in his pants he'd been sleeping in. "Go back to bed. I'll start the coffee urn. We may have company to take care of soon."

As Ross started the coffee, he remembered a prime directive from his training. One of the jobs of the rangers along the Appalachian Trail was to aid the hikers along the 2,160-mile path through the Appalachian Mountains. The Trail began in Georgia and stretched all the way to Maine. Hikers from around the world stepped out of their real lives to spend six to nine months on the Trail, finding themselves, God, clarity, whatever one found alone in the beauty of nature. Some only did a portion of the Trail during the summer. Some were diehards who challenged themselves to finish the entire journey without any outside help. Most were ordinary folks who would wake under an icy tent, cold, alone, and wondering why they were still out there in this weather. Those hikers would find their way to the Chattahoochee Forest Station needing help. Maybe some of them could help him move the tree off his truck and Felicity's vehicle.

Ross leaned back against the kitchen counter and closed his eyes. It would be easy to fall back to sleep as the coffee perked away. What he needed was coffee and Dorie.

Dorie! She shouldn't drive the mountain road today. When he looked out the window, it was still sleeting but changing over to snow. It looked like a major weather event.

Four a.m. He dialed Dorie anyway.

"Hello, Ross? What's happening?"

Her sleepy voice matched his sleepy eyes. "G'morning, Darlin'." Ross longed to take her in his arms. "Two things you need to know. First, you shouldn't drive the mountain road today. We're having a major winter storm. Second, my new truck is under a tree that fell on it this morning."

"Oh no! How will you get home?" Dorie sounded awake now. "I'm sure Riley will let me work from home. How's Felicity?"

"Her car is crushed under the tree too. We're fine, but we'll probably have a lot of hikers show up today. I've got the 60-cup urn perking."

"That's a lot of coffee, Ross. Be careful you don't drink more than you should."

"Is there a limit to my coffee consumption? Not like I'm sleeping well here anyway. The couch is, well, uncomfortable." Ross worried about Dorie's response to the sleeping arrangements.

"You're not sleeping in the bed?"

"I'm not sleeping in the bunkroom with Felicity. No reason to tempt jealousy from my new wife. You know, avoid the appearance of evil." Ross held his breath for her response.

"I trust you. You need sleep if you're going to come toe to toe with bears and lift trees off vehicles."

"And a lot of coffee. I better go. I love you, Dorie."

"I love you, too, Ranger Ross. Be safe. Don't worry. I'll be at home today." She hung up.

Ross longed for her touch, her kiss. He'd see her tomorrow night.

"Was that your wifey, Ross?"

Felicity startled him. "Yes, her name is Dorie." He thought about telling her what Dorie was working on, but he decided it might be proprietary. He pulled out his phone and showed her a picture of Dorie in Edinburgh. "On our honeymoon last week."

Felicity looked hard at the phone. "She seems familiar. Do I know her?"

Such a good question. Ross decided the simple truth was better than the convoluted version. "Dorie said you and she were similar looking. She works at Daelin PD, but before that, she worked at the *Daelin Beacon*."

"Hmm. Guess not." Felicity had dressed in uniform while Ross had set up the urn and called Dorie. She popped a decaf k-cup into the Keurig. "Supposed to avoid caffeine while I'm, you know."

Ross nodded like he knew these things. Without caffeine, Dorie might go stark, raving mad being pregnant.

Both of them jumped at a rap at the door and a call out. "Hello, anyone here?"

"I got it!" Felicity got a flying start and ended up in the front office before Ross.

The snowy hiker stamped his boots on the mat and stripped off his cap and scarf, flinging snow and ice onto the floor. He took off his coat and hung all of his outerwear on a hook by the door.

"Hi, you doing okay?" Felicity nearly fell into the man with Ross at her back. "We have coffee brewing."

Ross stopped himself before tripping over his partner.

"You guys know there's a tree on your vehicles?" He smoothed his beard of its icicles. "Coffee sounds like a good idea. Howard Waters is my name."

Ross reached around Felicity and shook Howard's hand. "Coffee's in the kitchen along with all the fixings. Welcome."

"Speaking of the tree, could you help us move it later, after you've warmed up?" Felicity headed to her computer and sat behind the desk. "Howard Waters, check."

"No problem. Maybe I'm a fool, but I didn't expect this weather last night." Howard wrapped his arms around himself and his layers of thermal and flannel clothing. "Especially in Georgia."

"I'm going to put in a call to the main station to let them know what happened to our cars and have no vehicular transportation." Felicity already had the phone to her ear.

Ross nodded. The he showed Howard Waters back to the kitchen. He heard the door open again. Yep, it was going to be a busy day.

Dorie caught her breath as she let Star out into the back. The trees glistened in the early dawn light with the coating of ice and the flocking of snow. Star slid more than ran around the yard, did her business, and hurried back into the garage. She shook and stretched, then trotted into the warm house.

Dorie pulled on the heavy wool cabled sweater she'd bought in Scotland. Today was the perfect day for it. Coffee was the next necessity. Then she'd need to phone Riley. Before she'd fixed her coffee, her phone rang.

"Hello, Riley. I was just about to call."

"Stay where you are. It's treacherous on the mountain road." He was gasping and panting. "Jenny's car went off the road. They've taken her on to Daelin Medical. I think she's okay. I'll call with an update when I know something."

"Where are you?" Dorie could hear sirens and crunching ice in the background.

"Directing traffic until Junior gets up the road. I'm not kidding. Dorie. Stay put. Gotta go."

He hung up before she could say good-bye. Jenny going off the mountain road. That was an ironic situation if she really was her sister. Dorie dialed the medical center.

"Information," intoned the operator. "How can I help?"

"Hi, Dorie MacAvoy, Liaison Officer from Daelin PD. I understand that Jenny Schaefer is on her way there in an ambulance. Do you have any information about her condition?"

"Hello, Miss Dorie. It's JoAnn from church volunteering on phones." She chuckled. "I don't have info on Miss Jenny yet, but she has been entered into the computer. That means she's arrived. I'll give you a call back when I know something."

Should she go down the mountain to Daelin to be with Jenny?

Chapter 17
Cleaning up from the snow event …

Ross and Riley had been perfectly clear. Do not leave the house in this dangerous icy snowstorm. Dorie wanted to be with Jenny. After all, she might be her sister. Dorie pondered her options as she sipped her coffee and ate some toast. Despite her pondering, she couldn't see an exception that would allow her to head down the mountain.

Her phone rang. Daelin Medical Center.

"Hello?"

"Miss Dorie, this is JoAnn. I personally checked on Jenny Schaefer. She's got a bump on her head and some bruises. I told her you called to check on her. She was quite touched and wanted me to thank you."

"Thanks for getting back to me. Will she stay in the hospital?"

"No, they're releasing her, and Captain McDonough is picking her up."

Dorie sighed with relief. "Thanks for checking on her, JoAnn."

She hung up and opened her laptop. She'd see what she could find about her biological mom and her sisters on Google.

Ross could barely move his muscular 6'4" body through the crowd of men and women hikers. He'd already perked a second urn full of coffee. Felicity was holding court in the kitchen. No sign of nausea today. The men wouldn't be nearly so interested if they knew she was pregnant. He grabbed his coat from its hook, and with chain saw in hand, he went outside to survey the damage to his truck. Howard Waters followed him out.

The snow had stopped, and the forest had a muffled silence about it. The birds chirped in the sun. Ross and Howard surveyed the tree and determined that moving the tree. as is, was an impossibility. Ross cranked up the chainsaw and cut the tree in half between the two vehicles. Then he cut the top of the tree as near as he could to Felicity's car. Howard was able to move the resulting log off of the red hatchback.

Ross cut another swath of the tree at the opposite side of his brand-new pickup truck. The remaining tree fell to the ground with an *oomph*. Howard helped him roll the section off the back of the truck. Then they hauled it to the side of the parking lot.

He ran his hand along the side of the pickup bed. Crushed described Ross's mood as well as the sides of the new truck. Unless it had damaged the suspension, it should be drivable though. Felicity's car was another situation. The tree had destroyed the body cavity of the front seat area. She'd need to call a tow truck and find another ride home. If Ross gave her a ride, perhaps this was a God-incident for

Felicity to meet Dorie.

Howard picked through the gear that had been dumped before entering the station. His stuff was at the bottom of the pile, of course. First in, last out, so to speak.

"Thanks for the coffee and warmup. I'd better get on my way to reach my next planned camp site." He shouldered his backpack with minimal camping supplies attached.

"Thanks for your help, Howard." Ross shook his hand and clapped him on the back. "Safe travels. Be careful of slick spots on the Trail."

When Ross turned back to the ranger station, he saw Felicity's look of horror when confronting the damage to her car.

"Oh, no! How will I get home?" The shriek threatened the silence of the woods.

"I'll drive you home. Check with your insurance company and have it towed to your car repair shop. In fact, why don't you come home with me tomorrow night for dinner, meet Dorie, and I'll get you home?" Ross walked to her side as the tears rolled down her cheeks.

"I don't have accident insurance, only liability."

Ross guided her back to the warmth of the station as the rest of the hikers trooped out into the weather. "Call your husband. He can come and see what you can do."

Felicity swiped the tears from her face. "It's just me and baby. There's no husband, boyfriend, or anyone else. It's just me. With no car." She stomped into the bunkroom and slammed the door.

One of the hikers stopped and stared at Ross.

"What'd you say to her? You should fix that."

Ross grimaced. "It's not about me, for a change. Bet I'm going to pay for it anyway, if it's anything like it is with my wife."

"She's not your wife?"

"No, I just met her this week." Ross shook off his coat and hung it up. "It's complicated." *And you can't imagine the half of it.* "Be safe out there."

"And to you, too." The man laughed and smirked. "I'd rather tackle the Trail than an upset lady."

Ross chuckled quietly, so Felicity wouldn't hear. He nodded and fist bumped the last hiker. Once he left, Ross headed back to the kitchen to clean up the mess.

Felicity joined him in the kitchen and perched on the stool. "Sorry for that temper tantrum. Guess it's the hormones. Either way, it's not your fault. Is that opportunity to meet your wife still on the table?"

Ross laughed. "After I check with her. She may have to come get us if my suspension's shot."

Dorie was surfing the web, following rabbit trails, when Riley rang.

"Dorie, I've got Jenny with me. She's under concussion protocol for today and tomorrow. I wondered if she could come stay with you today. Ross is in the forest, right?"

"I'm here by myself, yes. She's welcome to come." Dorie looked around to see if anything was out of place.

"Great, I'd watch over her myself, but the roads are creating mayhem. Her Aunt Flo is supposed to have an inspection today. On top of that, some folks have lost power and started their gas-driven generators. Two people have died for not venting the emissions properly."

"Oh, no. Sounds like it's a busy day. I feel like I'm playing hooky." Dorie checked the guest room to be sure the bed was made up since her family had been there.

"No need for that. Your boss and your husband told you to stay home. You are able to work from home. Today you may as well. I'll be there shortly."

Riley hung up before Dorie could say good-bye. He was clearly stressed. If taking care of Jenny helped him, she could do that. And she could get to know her as well.

Dorie started a full pot of coffee and got out a package of chocolate chunk cookies. She stopped short of plating the store-bought cookies, like so many Southern hostesses would.

Chapter 18
Getting to know you …

Dorie was wiping down the guest bathroom when she heard Riley's rap at the door and his "Hello?"

She leaned over the railing and called out. "Come in. I'll be right down." Dorie double checked the bathroom, then she headed down the stairs.

"Welcome. Oh, Jenny, your poor head!"

Not only did Jenny have two black eyes, but she also had a knot the size and color of a plum on her forehead. Her right arm was bound up in a sling.

She carefully hugged her and took her coat.

"I smell coffee. Can I get you a cup, Jenny?" Riley took her gloves and scarf.

"No, I think I need to lie down. Is that okay, Dorie?"

"That's fine, Jenny. Let me show you the guest room."

"I'm sorry to impose, but Aunt Flo is having the B & B inspected by the state today. Last thing she needs to worry about is me."

Dorie showed her the room. "Go ahead and get comfy. Pull back the covers. I'll check on you in an hour." She closed the door and checked her watch. Ten o'clock.

Riley was at the bottom of the stairs. "Is she okay?"

"I'm sure she will be. She needs rest as much as anything. I'll take care of her."

Riley nodded. "Thanks. I better get back out there."

Dorie scoured the internet, looking for mentions of Selene Mackenzie, the accident, the three little girls, anything. She checked in on Jenny at 11 and 12. As she was fixing lunch, Jenny appeared at her elbow.

"Hey, lunch sounds like a good idea. The pain killers are bouncing around in my stomach."

Dorie gave her what she hoped was a reassuring smile. "Absolutely. Will peanut butter do or would you like some soup?"

"Peanut butter will be fine." Jenny winced as she adjusted her sling. "I'm pretty easy to please, in general. What have you been up to while I've been doing my Sleeping Beauty impression?"

Dorie pulled out two more slices of bread and passed the peanut butter to Jenny. "Can you do it or should I? I'll warn you. I like raisins on my peanut butter sandwich."

Jenny's face lit up. "Me too! I've never found anyone else who did."

Dorie took back the peanut butter, spread it on the slices of bread, then sprinkled two of the slices with raisins. She cut both sandwiches diagonally.

"Ooh, that's my favorite too. It tastes better cut

diagonally." Jenny's smile was as wide as it could be, considering the bruising and swelling on her face.

"Right? My family always tells me I'm crazy." *Of course, they're not my biological family, are they?* "Coffee, Coke, or tea?"

"Tea sounds soothing. I'm already tired even though I haven't done anything." Jenny sat at the two-person bistro table in the kitchen.

Dorie started water to heat in the tea kettle and poured herself another cup of coffee. "Blackberry Sage tea?"

"That sounds divine."

Dorie prepared the mug for Jenny. "Sugar?"

"Just a scant teaspoon."

When the kettle screamed, Dorie poured the hot water into the mug and brought it to Jenny.

"You are so kind to watch over me today. I told Riley I didn't need a babysitter. Maybe he was right to insist." Jenny took a sip of the tea after waiting for it to brew. "That is amazing, Dorie. Thank you."

They fell into easy conversation. Dorie had questions she wanted to ask Jenny about their mom, foster care, Felicity. She also didn't want to take advantage of Jenny's injuries to pump her for information.

"I recently found out that my family is not my family." Dorie waited to see Jenny's reaction. "It appears I'm adopted."

"You were a lucky one. Foster care is not for the faint of heart." Jenny sipped her tea. "Some of the foster parents treat you like their own child, but some see a foster kid as a paycheck."

"That's horrible."

"What's worse is that the less they spend on you, the more profit they make. You sometimes don't get good food, clothing, shoes, or toys because the foster parents are using the money to cover their own vices." Jenny stirred her tea absentmindedly. "You know, alcoholism, gambling, internet porn. I learned a lot about people bouncing around the foster care system."

"How old were you when you entered the system?" Dorie didn't want to pry. She just wanted some confirmation of what she'd found.

"Three. My father was already dead. I had two sisters, one younger and one older. We were in a car accident, like the one I had today. I'm so grateful for airbags! Maybe if my mom had had airbags, they would have saved her life." A tear came to her eye and ran down her face.

"Do you remember your mom and sisters?" Dorie didn't want to be too bold until she knew for sure.

"I do, some, anyway. I'll never forget the accident." Jenny swirled the teabag in her cup with a spoon. "Mom was named Selene. My sisters were Felicity and Dorene. Dorene was the baby. Everything else is a blur."

"Wow." Dorie had already opened that door. It was time to step through it and claim herself. "My name is Dorene Annalise."

"Seriously?" Jenny grabbed Dorie's hand. "Are you my baby sister?"

Dorie shrugged. "I might be. And Ross is working with a lady named Felicity."

"I can't believe it! What are the odds that we'd

find each other in the same place?"

"Probably slim. We need to determine the truth. Check DNA, for instance." Dorie wasn't sure what more she should tell her. She wasn't at liberty to discuss the case with her. That much she knew. "How are you feeling?"

"Better, but I should probably lay back down." Jenny rose from the table. "I still can't believe it!" Jenny gave her a hard hug.

"I'll check on you in an hour, okay?" Dorie hugged her back.

Dorie's phone rang. Jenny headed back to the bedroom as Dorie answered the phone.

"Ross! Everything going okay?"

"Depends on what you mean by everything. The truck needs repair. I'm hoping it's drivable." Ross described the tree and its damage to both his new truck and Felicity's car.

"I'm so sorry. Your brand-new truck!" Dorie was concerned about the truck but more concerned for Ross, his safety, and his ability to come home.

"We've been swamped with hikers trying to find refuge for an hour or two due to the weather. One of them helped me get the tree off the vehicles."

"I have a refugee here too. Jenny went off the road close to where the accident happened twenty some years ago. Luckily, the airbags went off, but her face is bruised and swollen. She's in the guest bedroom under concussion protocol." Dorie paused. "Ross, she remembers the accident and her two sisters."

"Whoa, that's some break-through, Sweetheart. Hey, I must drive Felicity home tomorrow. How do you feel about having Felicity over for dinner tomorrow night?"

"I would love to meet her. I'm more than convinced that she's my second sister." Dorie's butterflies in her stomach made her nauseous. Two sisters. "I bet Jenny would want to be here too."

"Invite Riley and Jenny then. We should be there by five-ish tomorrow. I love you."

After Ross hung up, Dorie's sense of self rocked. She rushed to the bathroom and threw up her lunch.

"Are you okay, Dorie?" Jenny stood behind her. She wrapped her arms around Dorie. "Is everything okay?"

"Yes, I just became quite ill." Dorie sighed. Perhaps there was more to it, but she had no proof of that. "I think I'll lie down for a bit. Ross has invited Felicity to dinner tomorrow evening. Would you and Riley care to come, too?" Dorie stood.

"Three of us together again? I can't believe it." Jenny hugged her tight and then walked with her to her bedroom. "Thank you. I wouldn't miss the opportunity to be here."

Chapter 19
The red car …

The next day, once the ice was melting, Ross called Angela's husband George to bring his tow truck up the mountain to get Felicity's car. He towed it to his garage for an estimate for repairs. When their shift had ended, and the next unit had come on duty, Ross went out and started his truck. He put it in reverse, and the truck moved.

"Praise God! The truck will get us down the mountain."

Felicity climbed into the cab with her things. "Thank you, Ross. I look forward to visiting with your wife."

Ross turned the truck down the road. The suspension was rough, but it would get him home. And back to his Dorie. She'd sounded weak when he'd spoken to her last night. He was worried that she was not okay.

He turned the truck into the yard.

"Oh, Ross, what a lovely house." Felicity put her hand on his arm. "You are a lucky man."

"I know. Wait until you meet my wife." Ross carefully removed Felicity's hand. "She's a lovely lady. And I love her."

Felicity nodded and withdrew her hand. "I understand."

Ross climbed out of the truck and headed toward the front door, which opened as soon as he touched the ground.

Dorie ran out of the house and into his open arms. "Ross, I am so glad to have you home."

He picked her up and hugged her to him. "I love you, Dorie. Wherever you are is my home. I miss you so much when I'm gone."

She threw her arms around his neck. "I love you, Ross." She buried her face in his neck. Tears ran down her face and into his shirt. "I've been sick. I think I might be …"

"Hush, it's okay. We've got company." Ross set her back down on her feet. "Dorie, this is Felicity. Felicity, this is my wife, Dorie."

"Hello, Felicity, please come in out of the cold." Dorie hugged her and led her into the house.

Jenny waited at the door and hugged Felicity as she entered. "Do you remember us? Jenny and Dorene?"

"What?" Felicity turned to Ross and Dorie and back to Jenny. "Do you mean, you're my sisters?"

Riley joined the crew at the front door. "You must be Felicity. Why don't we all get in the house?"

Ross herded the crowd into the house. The warmth and the smell of pot roast welcomed him home too. "It smells great in here. Did you use the Crockpot?"

Felicity looked from Jenny to Dorie. "Oh my. I've been looking for the two of you for forever." She gathered them into her arms.

Riley shook Ross's hand. "Good to see you, man."

"Absolutely." Ross turned and looked at the three ladies. "They have to be sisters. They're the same height. They even look a lot alike."

"Frightening, isn't it?" Riley backed away to avoid the 'buddy punch' he expected from Ross.

"Yes, actually, it is frightening. I live with one and work with another."

"I know. I'm dating one and working with the other, my friend."

Ross picked up his duffle bag and headed up the stairs to his bedroom. He unpacked the dirty clothes and hung up what was left. The feminine squeals found their way up the stairs. He shook his head.

"Hey, stranger."

Ross turned around and found Dorie in the doorway. He hurried to her in two steps and held her to him. "Ah, Darlin', I missed you so much."

They sat wrapped together on the edge of the bed.

"Are you okay, Love? I know that it's been a difficult, overwhelming time."

"Better now that you're here. I'm sorry about the truck."

Ross chuckled. "It got me home. That's all I needed."

"Oh, host and hostess! Is there something we need to do to eat sooner than later?" Riley's voice interrupted their reunion.

"Guess I better go finish dinner for our guests, though I'm still nauseous."

"Go on. I'll change and come down to help."

After Dorie left, Ross noticed the crumpled bed and mashed pillow. *She must feel bad to lie down two days in a row. Must be a stomach bug.*

Dorie descended the staircase, but the smell of food turned her stomach. Guests needed to be fed. *It's probably something I ate.* All she really wanted was to climb in bed and snuggle up with Ross for the night.

Jenny and Felicity accosted her at the bottom of the stairs.

"Felicity likes raisins on her peanut butter sandwiches too." Jenny hugged Felicity and then Dorie. "It must have been something our mom liked."

Dorie put on a brave smile while the ladies ran off to a corner to talk leaving Riley and Dorie alone.

"Want to help serve dinner, Riley?"

"Sure thing, until Ross comes down. I know y'all like to do that together." Riley joined her in the kitchen. "You look pretty tired, Dorie. Should you go sit down and put your feet up? Come to think of it, I didn't see much of you today at the department."

Dorie shook her head. "I hid in my office most of the day."

Riley put his hand on her forehead. "You don't seem warm. Are you sick? Are we all going to get sick after eating here tonight?"

"I don't think what's wrong with me is catching." Dorie opened the Crockpot, and the steam and aroma of roast beef saturated the air. "Riley, can you pull out the roast and potatoes and put them on the platter. Carve it up. I'll be back."

Dorie ran for the bathroom, making it just in time. She sat down on the bathroom floor and leaned against the wall. She had to be … All she wanted was a Coke.

Ross opened the door. "You okay, Darlin'?" He handed her a Coke.

"Are you reading my mind now?" Dorie popped the top and drank a sip.

"No, learning about pregnant women from my co-worker." He came on in and leaned against the opposite wall. "Felicity spends most of the mornings in the bathroom. All she wants is crackers and a Coke. I figured this might help."

"I don't know that I'm pregnant. The tests Chloe ran were negative. Wait. Felicity is pregnant? What are the odds?" Dorie laughed. "Wait, Felicity is pregnant? That's not good. Our break-in and hit-and-run suspect has my familial DNA and is pregnant."

"Uh, oh. What color was the car in the hit-and-run? Was it red?"

Dorie nodded. "We should tell Riley. Where's her car now?"

"George's shop." Ross helped Dorie up off the floor. "Are you okay?"

"Maybe. I left Riley finishing dinner."

Ross pulled her into his arms. "I love you. We might be pregnant?"

Dorie shrugged. "Either that or it's the flu, and I'm infecting all of you."

"I am up for either, but maybe not for the flu,

y'know?" Ross did his signature eyebrow wangle.

Dorie laughed.

A rap at the door startled them into peals of laughter.

Riley called out to them. "Guys, dinner's on the table. You coming?"

Ross opened the door. "We're coming. Dorie wasn't feeling well."

Dorie grabbed Riley's wrist. "I need to tell you something. Felicity's car is red. And she's probably my sister."

"Is this the car that was smashed by the tree that they're talking about?" Riley frowned. "Where is it?"

"I had it towed to George's shop to assess whether it's fixable."

Riley nodded. "We have an APB for shop owners to watch for a red car with suspicious damage. George will call me if it's the car we're looking for."

"I'm going to go lie down. You guys go ahead and eat. Come get me when it's time for dessert." Dorie slipped upstairs.

Ross became the host of the meal, so he made sure everyone had everything they needed. Jenny and Felicity chattered nonstop. *I wish Dorie had felt well enough to stay to hear the family talk that he was experiencing. I need to remember this for her.*

The sisters began clearing the table and setting out plates for dessert.

Ross hurried up the stairs to check on Dorie.

He knelt beside the bed. "Darlin', the food is put away and everyone is waiting for dessert. Are you feeling better?"

Dorie turned over toward him. "I think I can handle some vanilla ice cream. Perhaps we can save a piece of the apple pie for me for tomorrow."

"Come then. Let's serve our guests." Ross gave her his hand to help her up from the bed.

As Ross and Dorie worked on cutting and serving the pie, Riley's phone rang. Once he hung up, he corralled Dorie in the kitchen.

"We have an issue. George has just reported that Felicity's red car has a dent that has nothing to do with a tree falling on it. It also has a bit of blood on it, hard to see on a red car. Forensics is at George's garage now going over it now. I need to arrest her and take her in."

"No! She has blonde hair, not brown." Dorie felt the tears prickle her eyes. "Darn emotions!" She swiped at the tears that fell.

Ross put his arm around her. "It'll be okay, Darlin'. If she's innocent, it will come to light."

"Can you guys get Jenny home?" Riley touched Dorie's shoulder. "It will all come out in the wash."

Dorie nodded and leaned into Ross. "I just got my sisters back. I didn't even know they existed until recently."

"Think about Todd Wilkins's family. They need closure." Riley headed for the dining room.

Ross and Dorie followed Riley to the table.

Riley took out his handcuffs. "Felicity Johnson, I'm arresting you on suspicion of vehicular manslaughter, leaving the scene of an accident, and at least three burglaries. You have the right to remain silent. Anything you say can be used against you in court. You have the right to talk to a lawyer for advice before we ask you any questions. You have the right to have a lawyer with you during questioning. If you cannot afford a lawyer, one will be appointed for you before any questioning if you wish. If you decide to answer questions now without a lawyer present, you have the right to stop answering at any time."

"I didn't kill anyone with my car! What makes you think I did?" Tears streamed down Felicity's face.

Dorie held her before Riley could put the cuffs on her. "When your car was delivered to George, he noticed you had a dent in the front of your car with blood in it. We had an APB out for any red cars with suspicious damage. So, George reported it when it was brought in."

Riley gently pulled Dorie away from Felicity. "Forensics has been all over your car. We're just waiting for a DNA match. I think it is Todd Wilkins's blood. We'll also check for fingerprints."

"I have a truck I drive too. In fact, I drove it last week to the ranger station."

"I'm sorry, ladies."

By then, all three women were in tears. Ross wrapped his arms around Dorie and held her. Jenny held on to Dorie's hand.

The click of the handcuffs had a finality to it.

Chapter 20
Tests for proof …

It was five in the morning when Ross awoke and realized Dorie was not beside him. He rose, slipped on his sweats, and walked through the cool upstairs, looking for her. Not finding her, he slipped quietly down the stairs where he found her asleep on the sofa. He slipped in under her and cradled her in his arms. She weighed nothing compared to his girth. And she was everything to him.

He was nearly asleep himself when Dorie woke.

"I had hoped not to wake you." She kissed him.

"You didn't. I just realized you weren't in the bed, so I came to find you." Ross brushed her auburn hair back from her face. "Are you okay?"

"You mean, am I still sick?" Dorie looked into his eyes. "Yes, deathly ill. I'll take a test today to see if it's, you know."

He closed his eyes and held her to him. "I don't want you to be ill for nine months, Darlin'."

"Most people get over it by the end of the first three months." She kissed him.

"Three months of feeling ghastly. That's ridiculous." He kissed her. "If I could take it from you and bear it myself, I would.”

“I’m sure you would, my love. Can I fix you coffee?”

Ross laid her on the sofa and rose. “I can make the coffee. You rest.”

Dorie’s phone rang. Ross picked it up. “Hello, Riley. What’s going on?” Ross put it on speaker. “You’re on speaker, and Dorie’s with me.”

“We have Jenny’s DNA and fingerprint analysis. Her DNA is a familial match to Dorie’s and to the suspect. We’ve taken DNA from Felicity and fingerprints. We’re running the blood from the car for DNA, as well.”

Dorie groaned. “I just got a sister and now she’s being taken from us.”

“Dorie, we’ll do what we have to do, nothing more. How are you feeling today?”

Dorie shook her head.

“She’s not great, Riley. We’re thinking she might be pregnant. By the way, Felicity is also pregnant. Treat her well, my friend.”

“Stay home today, Dorie. Take care of you. Go to the doctor and confirm what’s going on.”

“I’m home today. I’ll take care of her.” Ross rubbed her neck. “Bye.”

The coffee machine beeped. Ross hurried into the kitchen to fix Dorie’s coffee. He also fixed her some toast.

“Here you go, Darlin’. Coffee and toast.”

Dorie scooted into the corner of the sofa, wrapped in a blanket. She took the coffee mug and took a sip. “Wonderful.”

Ross curled up around her. “Ah, Darlin’, we’ll

get through this too. We've experienced so much. This is a reason to rejoice despite the rough beginning."

Dorie nodded. "As long as you walk through it with me."

"Where else would I be?"

Later that morning, Dorie insisted on going into work to check on Felicity while Ross took his truck to George's garage. He would walk back to Daelin PD after getting his truck evaluated. As long as he was off, they could get by with only one vehicle. What would happen if Felicity couldn't go to work? Ross would need another forest ranger with which to share duties. If he didn't have a vehicle? He'd need to rent one, Dorie supposed.

Dorie slipped downstairs to the Crime Lab.

"Chloe?" The lab was a little freaky when deserted. The morgue was down here too, though they rarely had "guests." "Are you down here?"

"Dorie, good to see you."

She startled at Chloe's greeting from behind her.

"You gave me a fright, girlfriend."

Chloe grinned. "What can I help you with?"

Dorie caught her breath. "Pregnancy test?"

"Really? The one I did a week or so ago was negative."

"How soon are those accurate? My morning sickness and exhaustion say otherwise." Dorie slipped into a blood draw chair.

"Usually, the first day you've missed a period

they are 99% accurate." Chloe gathered the tubes and syringes to draw blood. "Before that only 76% five days before your period would begin. I'd say if you're having symptoms, it's likely you're pregnant."

That made Dorie's head spin. Pregnant? Having a baby? She guessed they did everything faster than most couples. They fell in love quickly. Got married within six months of meeting. It only made sense that they'd become pregnant as soon as they were married.

"… so, I'll send this blood sample off. I should get the results tomorrow." Chloe had been talking without her even hearing her. "Why don't you go ahead and do a urine test?" She handed her a box for an at-home pregnancy test.

"Thanks, Chloe. Ross will probably be here at lunch. I think we'll have a lot to talk about." Dorie stood, and the room looped around her.

"Dizziness is an early sign of pregnancy too. Take extra care, okay?" Chloe embraced her. "You really do have signs of pregnancy. When's your period due?"

"This weekend."

Chloe nodded. "Let me know your results."

Dorie stopped in the restroom on her way back to her office. She did the urine test then put the stick back in the box to check later. After stashing the test in her purse, she went to her office.

Riley dropped in about the time she sat at her desk. "So you came in anyway. I was just going to question Felicity. Since you're here, I'd like you to watch and listen to see what connects to your research. Her fingerprints were a match to the ones we got at one of the churches. Still waiting on DNA on Jenny and Felicity."

"What about the car? Anything probative there?"

"You know forensics. Lots of data but not enough and not all related." Riley came in and sat beside her desk. "Are you feeling better?"

"I am for now. Chloe ran another test but won't know anything until tomorrow."

The test in her purse called out to her, *Check me, check me.* And even though the waiting time had passed and Dorie was tempted to peek, she wanted to share it with Ross later.

Dorie picked up her laptop, a legal pad, and a pencil. "Let's do this."

Dorie went into the control booth. Jordy joined her while Matt and Riley sat on the other side of the two-way mirror.

"Hey, Dorie. Is it true the suspect is your sister?" Jordy set up his space beside her with his coffee and a legal pad.

"So, it seems. Man, I forgot my coffee." Dorie knew this hi-test coffee could be her last. She was determined to enjoy it. When she stood, she wavered with another bout of dizziness.

"You sit. I'll go get your coffee." Jordy waited until she had successfully seated herself. Then he dashed from the room to find her coffee Thermos and mug.

While Dorie waited for him, an officer brought Felicity into the room with Riley and Matt and stayed at the door. Felicity was dressed in a Daelin PD sweatshirt and pants. The evidence of Felicity's pregnancy was visible in the loose clothing. Dorie touched her abdomen.

"Here ya go, Dorie-girl." Jordy crashed into the booth with her mug and coffee.

Dorie moved her hand back to the desk. "Thank you." She poured the steaming drink into the mug while Riley set up the recording equipment.

"Felicity Johnson is in the room with Captain Riley McDonough, Detective Matt Akers, and court appointed attorney Brian Griffith. Detective Jordan Mavers and Liaison Officer Dorie MacAvoy are listening in the booth. Ms. Johnson, is it true that you have been breaking into churches in Daelin?"

"Yes, sir."

"What was the purpose of the break-ins?"

"I was looking for records of my sisters." Felicity put her hands over her face. "That's all I was doing. Trying to find my sisters."

"Surely there were other means to find your sisters."

"I was adopted by family but no longer a Mackenzie. I tried searching by last name. No luck. The foster care system wouldn't help me. Adoption records were sealed. I know we went to church as children. I knew Mom was a member of some church."

"What about your red car? Did you drive the red car on Tuesday last?"

"No, I was at the ranger station with Dorie's husband Ross. I had taken my pickup truck to the station. I swear it. I did not use my car on last Tuesday. I did not kill the boy. You can ask Ross."

"Then who would have been driving your red car?"

Felicity shuddered. "I do not know. I was not there."

"Who has access to your red car besides you, Ms. Johnson?"

Felicity broke down and cried. "I don't want to say. I don't want to believe that she …"

"Who?" Riley took her hand.

The attorney spoke in her ear.

"Captain, Ms. Johnson believes she knows who the responsible party is. However, she wants to protect this person."

"Except for the broken glass and mayhem, the burglaries are misdemeanors." Detective Akers wrote a note on his notepad "We might be open to a deal for her information."

"I can't tell you before talking to Jenny and Dorie." Felicity laid her head in her hands on the table.

The attorney shrugged. "Can we get these two ladies here?"

Detective Akers pointed at the two-way mirror. "Dorie's in the booth behind the glass."

"I'll call Jenny. Recording ended at twelve-o-one." Riley switched off the recorder and whipped out his phone. "Just rest here for a minute. Dorie, come and sit with Felicity."

Dorie jumped up and met Riley in the hall.

"Be careful what she discloses to you. You are an officer of the court here. What you hear is lawfully accessible for court. Be sure she knows that she's technically on the record, even if the tape isn't running." He headed down the hallway to make his call to Jenny.

Chapter 21
More family secrets …

Dorie entered the interrogation room and sat across from Felicity. The lawyer and Matt scraped their chairs at a horrific shriek against the concrete floor.

"Dorie, you're here." She reached out and grabbed Dorie's hand. "This is such a mess."

"I've been here the whole time you've been questioned. Riley's calling Jenny. Do you need something to eat or drink?"

"Yes, maybe decaf coffee and something from a vending machine." Felicity wiped her face with her other hand.

"I bet we can do better than that." Dorie turned and faced the mirror. "Two café mochas, one decaf, and two chicken salad croissants from Java Joint, Detective Mavers?"

A tap on the glass affirmed the order.

"That's Angela's place, right? Her husband George was in my class at school." Felicity took a tissue from the box on the table and blew her nose. "They seemed like an unlikely pair in high school, but I guess they've got the real thing."

"What about you? Are you married? Your last name isn't Mackenzie either."

"No, but that's part of what I need to tell Jenny too, Let's talk about you. Ross is amazing and so sweet!"

Dorie sighed. "He is, and I've been jealous of all the days and nights he spends at the station with you."

"You needn't be. It's hard to look alluring when you're tossing your cookies and carrying another man's child." Felicity stroked the small mound in her abdomen.

Dorie resisted the urge to do the same. She didn't know yet. *I should have looked in the box.* But she really wanted to share that moment with Ross.

"When did you come back to Daelin? How did you and Ross meet?"

"It's a pretty short story. We haven't even known each other for a year. I moved here after finishing my journalism degree at Virginia Tech last May. Ross lived next door. I drenched him with coffee one Sunday on my way to church." Dorie laughed. "I will never live that down."

Felicity grinned. "Guess that got his attention."

"You could say that. After he changed, he took me to church with him."

"So, wait! You've only known each other…" She held up her hands and counted on her fingers. "June, July, August, September, October, November, December, January. Eight months!"

"Yep, we were married on Christmas Eve." Dorie nodded. "Not long at all. Do you want to see pictures?"

"No, no offense. Ross takes those photos out for every hiker that comes in. It's a wonder he hasn't posted a running slide show to our welcome screen." Felicity laughed. "He loves you so fiercely."

Dorie nodded. "I know, as I love him. It's probably not my business, but who's your baby's father? You don't have to tell me."

"No, you're my sister. He's a guy I'll never see again. We had dated for a while." Felicity wiped away a tear. "When the big snow happened the beginning of December, we were snowed in together. It was a party for a while. He turned out to be a jerk, especially once he found out I was pregnant."

A rap on the door startled them both. "Your order, madam."

The door opened as Dorie reached it. Jordy handed her a takeout bag and a drink carrier from Java Joint. "Jenny's just arrived too. I'll send her in."

"Sounds good. Thank you for getting lunch. I owe you."

Jordy nodded. "That you do, Mrs. MacAvoy."

Once he was gone, Dorie laughed. "He's not used to being an errand boy for the new civilian officer on the force."

"How do you do that? Get the men to do what you want?" Felicity mouth was open in amazement.

"I had three older brothers. I knew what gets them to do what they'd ordinarily not do." Dorie opened the chicken croissants, gave Felicity one, then bit into her own.

"That's how you got Ross?" Felicity took a bite of her croissant.

"No, that was mostly Ross." Dorie checked the

drinks and gave Felicity the one marked decaf. Then she took a sip of the other one.

The door opened again, and Jenny slipped into the interrogation room.

"I try hard not to ever end up in one of these rooms."

"Want part of my croissant, Jenny?" Dorie offered a piece she'd cut off the croissant.

"No, I already ate, and you're eating for two, after all."

Felicity laughed. "You're pregnant too?"

"Not confirmed yet. Why not just broadcast it to the world?"

"I can do that." Jenny laughed. "Just find out soon. I dying to find out if I get to be an aunt twice this fall."

When they finished laughing, Felicity turned serious.

"Dorie, I know you probably have to divulge what I say but give me a chance to explain."

Dorie nodded.

"Being the oldest, I remember the accident and being split apart from you two vividly. It's the one thing in my life that's defined me. Family means more to me than I can say. I was too young to look for you."

"At five? I'd think so." Jenny grabbed onto Felicity's hand. "I didn't know what happened to you either."

Dorie wanted so much to roll her eyes. She'd never known they existed. Until January! She was late to this family reunion. And still unsettled about the whole business. If she was pregnant, ... it just complicated the whole thing.

"Dorie, are you okay?" Felicity grabbed her hand.

"I didn't know any of this. I don't know what to say to either of you."

Jenny grabbed her other hand. "It's okay. You were a baby."

"Well, to continue my story, our mom has a sister. Jacqueline. Most folks call her Jac'line, you know, rhymes with Selene and each of one of our names." Felicity shook her head. "What I need to say is hard, ladies. So hard."

"Tell us, Felicity. We need to know." Jenny had a tear course down her cheek.

"Jac'line took me in, adopted, and raised me. But she didn't want any babies or toddlers. She was the one who put you two in foster care." Felicity paused.

"She didn't want her nieces?" Jenny took her hand from Felicity and grabbed a tissue. "I just can't believe that. Your children aren't even born, and I'd take them both if anything happened."

"Well, it wasn't butterflies and puppy dogs. Jac'line's husband beat her. All the time, sometimes for nothing. When I got old enough to understand, I stayed far away from him and tried to be quiet, so Aunt Jac'line wouldn't get beat. I also locked my bedroom door at night."

"Oh, Felicity!" Dorie was crying and needed the tissue box next.

Felicity shook her head. "Water under the bridge. He died when I was thirteen. I was always afraid Aunt Jac'line murdered him somehow, but I was also grateful he was no longer in the house at night, especially as I was entering puberty."

"So, you lived happily ever after, right?" Jenny brightened.

Dorie had written far too many sad family stories for the press to believe in happily ever after, excepting her and Ross, of course. "What happened, Felicity?"

"The doctors say that Jac'line's head has taken way too many blows. As I entered high school, she began forgetting things, driving crazy, saying things that just didn't make sense. It's that condition the football players get from being concussed so often. Long term brain damage. Chronic Traumatic Encephalopathy is the fancy word or CTE."

"What's that like?" Dorie took her hands back from her sisters and started taking notes.

"It's like dementia. She doesn't remember much of anything. She has horrific mood swings. Some days she doesn't even know me. She shouldn't drive." Felicity shuddered. "I bet she took my car when I was at work. I always hide the keys, but she must have found them." Tears flowed down Felicity's cheeks now. "What will they do to her?"

"Does she wear her hair in a light brown ponytail?" Dorie knew what the answer had to be, but she needed to firm up this info with the eyewitness testimony.

"When I'm not at the ranger station, I brush her hair and put it up in a ponytail, so it won't get all straggly and in her face." Felicity nodded. "Yes, her hair looks brown at a distance, but it's actually a combination of our hair, blonde, auburn, and light brown."

"Who takes care of her when you're at the ranger station?" Dorie nodded and wrote down the last of it.

"No one. She stays home when I'm gone." Felicity chewed her lip. "I know she needs care."

"I'll go talk to Riley. They won't send her to prison. She's not mentally competent to stand trial, in my opinion. Wait here."

She pressed in the code that unlocked the door and headed straight to Riley's office. She gathered Jordy and Matt on the way. When she reached the captain's office, she knocked on the heavy wood door.

"Come in!" came the reply.

Dorie opened the door. Jordy picked up a chair from the hall, so each of them had a place to sit.

"Well? You don't normally knock, Dorie. Guys, what's happening?" Riley stood then perched on his desk in front of them.

"Here's the fast and dirty version: I have an Aunt Jacqueline Johnson who took in Felicity after the accident with my mom. She was abused regularly by her husband and has permanent brain damage. The woman probably was the one driving Felicity's car while she was at the ranger station."

"You have two sisters and an aunt you didn't know about? That's amazing!" Matt laced his fingers and put them behind his head.

"Not the point, Matt." Riley sighed. "So, the woman isn't responsible for her actions, but also shouldn't be on the roads because she's a menace to society."

Dorie nodded.

"Jordy, get Felicity out of handcuffs and take her with you to pick up Jacqueline Johnson. Matt, you go with him. Ask her for the name of her aunt's doctor. Make sure she's safe with you."

Jordy nodded. "No problem, Captain."

The detectives jumped up from their chairs and headed back to the interrogation room.

Dorie leaned forward. "What do you want me to do, Riley?"

"Liaison. Call her doctor and substantiate all this info about the brain damage. If he won't talk to you due to HIPPA, bring him in, so Ms. Johnson can give him permission to talk to you." Riley pulled on his jacket. "I'm going to visit the district attorney and tell him about all this mess."

Chapter 22
Unraveling the mystery …

Dorie drove to the Medical Center to the offices of Dr. Harrison, Aunt Jac'line's neural doctor. She entered the office and spoke to the receptionist.

"How can I help you, love?" The receptionist smacked her gum.

"I need to see Dr. Harrison."

"Sweetheart, he has a backlog of two months. I can make you an appointment for April."

Dorie reached into her purse, touching the pregnancy test box. She startled and then pulled out her badge. "I don't think so. I'm Dorie MacAvoy, Liaison Officer for Daelin PD. I'm here on police business."

The receptionist sat up straight. "Well, why didn't you say so at the start?" She pressed a button on an intercom. "Dr. Harrison, the police are here for your help."

"Very well. Send him in."

"He's a she, sir."

"Very well."

The receptionist conducted Dorie to the doctor's

office. "Dorie MacAvoy, Liaison Officer from Daelin PD, Dr. Harrison."

The doctor stood and indicated a seat for Dorie.

She sat on the edge of the chair, not intending on being there long. "I'm a niece of Jac'line Johnson. She's suspected to have driven the car that killed Todd Wilkins. It's important for us to understand the neurological condition of Ms. Johnson."

"I'm sure you are aware that I cannot tell you anything about her condition without her permission."

Dorie nodded. "Then you need to accompany me to the station, so you can get her permission. You'll need to cancel your appointments for this afternoon. Please bring her file with you, to save time."

Ross walked into the PD station. The atmosphere was charged, but no excitement appeared on the surface. He waved at the desk sergeant and walked back toward Dorie's office. Not finding her there, he walked back to Riley's office. No one there either. He strolled back to the detectives' bullpen. No one there either.

"Hmm. Where is everyone?" A charge of fear ran up his arm. Something was going down somewhere. His wife and his best friend were in harm's way and not a thing he could do. His heart started beating faster.

"Ross! You're here." Dorie's voice came from behind him.

He turned and opened his arms just in time for her embrace. "Is everything okay?"

"Yes, I suppose. There's lots to tell you." She released Ross and turned to the stern-looking man carrying a briefcase who was following her. "Go to the end of this hall and wait at the door marked Interrogation #1. I'll be there in just a moment."

"Is everything okay?" He knew he was repeating himself, but if he asked again, perhaps she'd let him in on what was going on. "Is Felicity okay?"

"She's okay. Do you want to wait in the coffee break area? Or you could go to Java Joint for better coffee."

Ross held his stomach. "George and I just had lunch there. Angie just kept bringing us more coffee and more of this and more of that."

"So, you won't want dinner tonight, right?" Dorie grinned as she teased him.

His heart fluttered when she smiled at him like that. "I probably will be hungry again sometime." He kissed her. "The truck is toast, officially, by the way. I went looking at the car lot and tentatively chose something. We can go by and seal the deal on the way home."

Dorie kissed him. "I don't know how long this is going to take. Maybe you should go ahead and buy yourself that big bad truck you want. It really only affects me if you don't have it."

"Are you sure? I got in a lot of trouble the last time I bought vehicles without your approval." Ross looked down into her beautiful eyes. Who was he kidding, anyway? She owned him heart and soul and any other way but loose.

"Buy the truck you want, then come back here. Maybe we can both leave by then." She kissed him again and wriggled out of his embrace. "Whoever gets home first cooks or brings home carryout."

"You got it, wifey!" Ross backed down the hall, watching her hurry to the interrogation room.

"Watch out!"

Ross turned just in time to avoid running in to Riley and his cup of steaming, black coffee. "Sorry. I was just watching my wife."

"You do realize that I will never be able to marry any woman because you guys are so perfect together. I'll never find the 'one' as perfect for me." Riley sipped his coffee. "Sorry, I've got to go supervise this fiasco." He hurried off down the hall after Dorie.

For a moment, Ross felt utterly alone as the interrogation room acted like a black hole, sucking in all that dared to come near it. Then he realized, *I get to go buy a truck.* That was better any day than being in interrogation.

Dorie slipped into the room. Felicity was holding the hands of the woman she assumed to be her Aunt Jac'line. She spoke with her just out of Dorie's ability to understand her. Dr. Harrison sat beside her, checking Jac'line's pulse and heart. Jenny sat alone across the room. The detectives sat at the table with Riley. *Where do I belong?*

Jenny motioned for Dorie to join her. Grateful to be wanted somewhere, she crossed the room to Jenny's perch at the window.

"Thanks for coming over. I was feeling alone." Jenny crossed her legs and patted the chair beside her.

Dorie slipped into the chair. "Ross was here. I sent him out to buy a new truck."

"Sounds like he needed one. Just like Felicity needs a new car."

"At least she has her pickup." Dorie anxiously tapped her foot. "What are they doing?"

"Dr. Harrison declared that Jac'line is not fit for interrogation and is taking vital signs to prove it. Felicity is trying to calm her down, so she can answer questions." Jenny touched Dorie's arm. "I am ready to go back to Helen and help Aunt Flo clean bedrooms. I can't take this stress."

"You probably don't have to stay here. You're not guilty of anything except being related to us." Dorie laughed. "So far, that's not a crime."

Jenny threw her arms around Dorie. "I'm so glad you ended up back here with me and with Felicity. Such a coincidence."

"It's truly a God thing, isn't it?" Dorie hugged her back. "My favorite verse from the Bible is in the book Jeremiah. It says, 'I know the plans I have for you. Plans to give you a future and a hope.'"

"That sounds like something Riley would say. I wasn't raised in the church. Except for seeing the Gideon Bibles in the drawers of the guest rooms, I've never read the Bible." Jenny sat back down. "I'm beginning to think it's a deal breaker with Riley."

Dorie nodded. "It could be. The Bible teaches us that Christians should not partner with non-Christians."

"I have a feeling that's what Riley's about to say to me."

"Are you in love with him?" Dorie watched the group surrounding Jac'line. They seemed like there was motion toward the table.

"I don't know. It hasn't been that long that we've been dating. How did you and Ross fall in love so quickly?" Jenny swung her foot back and forth.

"It was a God thing." Dorie smiled, remembering their short courtship.

Riley jumped up and crossed the room to where Dorie and Jenny sat.

"Is Aunt Jac'line competent? I remember wondering why she didn't want me or Dorie. It hurt me." Jenny gritted her teeth. "Guess it was better she didn't take us."

"Sounds like, according to what Felicity described." Dorie hugged her.

"I'm going to need you back in the booth, Dorie. Jenny, you're going to need to leave. If you want to sit in my office, that's okay."

"Nah, I got to go in to work in just a bit." She stood and squeezed his hand. "See you later."

Riley nodded. "Okay."

Dorie got up and headed toward the booth, dragging Matt with her. "C'mon, Matt. Back to the penalty box."

"Wait, isn't interrogation the penalty box?"

Chapter 23
Getting to the truth …

Dorie poured the rest of her coffee from the Thermos into her VA Tech mug. Matt played with the adjustable chair, trying to get it to adjust. In the interrogation room, Riley set up the sound system. Felicity sat next to Aunt Jac'line with Dr. Harrison on the other side. Jordy stacked paper and tapped it to get the stack even on all sides.

"Ready, people?"

Riley seemed irked to Dorie. It had been a bit of a day. Hard to tell what was bothering him now. He switched on the recording device. Riley named all the people in the room as well as Dorie and Matt in the booth for the benefit of the recording.

"Miss Felicity Maxine Johnson, do you admit to the burglary of churches in the area?"

"Yes, sir. I was trying to find my sisters."

"Were you able to find your sisters? What are their names?" Riley shifted in his seat.

"Yes, I was. Jennifer Irene Schaefer and Dorene Annalise Hudson MacAvoy. We were all Mackenzies before we became wards of the state." Felicity grabbed a tissue from the box.

"What happened to you?" Riley drew on the paper in front of him.

"Our Aunt Jac'line took me in and adopted me." Felicity dabbed at her eyes. "It's not my fault she didn't want Jenny and Dorie."

"I couldn't take three girls." Jac'line leaned toward Riley. "I did the best I could for the oldest one. Little ones I couldn't do."

The attorney leaned forward. "Mrs. Johnson has nothing to say until you have a question for her."

Dr. Harrison raised his hand. "You have not determined whether Mrs. Johnson is able to answer your questions. Until I weigh in on competency, she should not be allowed to speak on the record."

"Hold on to your pants, guys. We're just trying to figure out what's happening." Jordy handed Jac'line a bottle of water. "Here. Let us talk to Felicity first. Then we'll have some questions for you."

"Thank you, Detective." She took the water and opened it.

Dorie jumped up and left the booth. She rushed to the interrogation room. "Let me talk with my Aunt Jac'line while you talk with Felicity."

Riley nodded. "Jac'line Johnson and Dorie MacAvoy are leaving the room."

Dorie took Jac'line to the coffee break room.

"Selene?" She gripped on to Dorie and wept.

"I'm Dorie, Aunt Jac'line."

"That's right, Selene died." She began to weep. "It was so hard losing my sister. I couldn't keep all three girls. Hugh was bad. I could protect one, but not three."

Dorie settled her back into a chair and knelt beside her. She brushed Jac'line's hair back from her eyes.

"You look so much like her. Selene had the most beautiful auburn hair growing up. And those same dark brown eyes." Tears ran down Jac'line's face. "I miss her all the time. What's your name again?"

"Dorie. Dorene Annalise."

"I begged her to name you Annalise. It's my middle name too."

Dorie jumped up and hugged Jac'line. "Then we share something very special, don't we?"

"Do we? It was Selene who had the auburn hair, not me." She looked up to Dorie, clear- eyed, childlike.

"How about a snack? Did you have lunch?" Dorie took Jac'line's hand and led her to the snack machine. "See what looks good while I go get my wallet."

Dorie hurried to her office and reached for her wallet. Her hand brushed the box. "Not now!" She said it aloud, so she wouldn't be tempted to look. She had other things to do and Ross to share it with. She took the wallet and headed back to the break room.

"They have Cheez-its. I love Cheez-its! Is it okay if I get Cheez-its, Sis?"

Dorie swallowed hard. No way was Jac'line competent or responsible for her actions. She couldn't hold a thought for a minute. Her prior injuries must have been severe.

"Yes, Jac'line, you can have Cheez-its." Dorie waved her credit card in front of the scanner and selected the snack she wanted. Then she waved it again and got a Mounds bar for herself.

"Can I have a candy too, Selene?" She scrunched her shoulders in a plea.

Dorie bought her a Mounds bar. They returned to the table with the bottle of water to eat their snacks. Dorie wished she had her coffee.

After a few minutes, Riley appeared and beckoned Dorie into the hallway.

"Well?" Riley rubbed his hand through his brown hair. "Is she competent?"

"No way. She can't hold a thought for longer than a minute or two. She thinks I'm her sister Selene because I have auburn hair. She understands when I tell her different, but the next time I see her, she thinks I'm Selene." Dorie offered him the second piece of her candy bar, which he took with delight.

"Thanks." He put the whole thing in his mouth, closed his eyes, and savored the dark chocolate and coconut. When he had finished, he turned to Jac'line. "We're ready to talk to you now, Mrs. Johnson."

"Can my sister come with me?" Jac'line stood and latched onto Dorie's arm.

"Sure." Riley shook his head as he walked down the hall toward interrogation. When they arrived at the door, he opened it with the code. Before Dorie could enter, he stopped her. "She's really this far 'round the bend?"

Dorie nodded. "I don't know what Dr. Harrison has to say, but there's no way she's competent to stand trial. I doubt she even remembers driving the car."

"Okay, let's finish this up so we can all go

home." Riley sighed and held the door for her.

After everyone was settled around the table, Riley started the recording again with a recitation of those present.

"Mrs. Johnson, do you sometimes drive Felicity's car?"

"No, the red car is mine. My husband bought it for me." Mrs. Johnson looked at all the people in the room. "I have a right to drive it if I want."

Dr. Harrison cleared his throat. "I have made it abundantly clear to both Mrs. Johnson and Ms. Johnson that Mrs. Johnson should not be driving."

"Doctor, can you explain why for the tape?" Riley tapped his pencil.

"Yes, Mrs. Johnson suffers from a brain injury caused by repeated head trauma at the hands of her abusive husband. My professional opinion is that she is incompetent to drive as well as incompetent to be tried for the crime we are discussing. I've have insisted multiple times that Mrs. Johnson be institutionalized for her sake as well as Ms. Johnson's sake."

"Felicity, why have you ignored your aunt's doctor?" Riley slid the pencil onto his ear.

"Money. I don't have any to commit her to a care facility. I'm home three nights and two days. I make sure she has food, clean clothes, errands accomplished before I go back on shift. Usually, she just watches television and sleeps while I'm at the station." She wrung her hands. "I had no idea she'd try to drive while I was gone."

"Mrs. Johnson, did you drive your red car last Tuesday?" Riley had started tapping on the table with his finger.

"I don't know what day it was."

"Did you hit a young boy on his bicycle while driving your red car?"

Jac'line's hands began to shake. "He fell off his bike like I scared him. I backed up to check on him. He wouldn't answer. He was trying to trick me to get out of the car."

"Then what happened?"

"I went home. I knew Felicity would be mad that I went out without her, but I wanted a chocolate milk shake real bad."

Felicity took Jac'line's hand. Tears streamed down Felicity's cheeks.

"I'm sorry. I made you cry. I won't do it again."

Riley stood. "Wait here. I'll go talk to the prosecutor."

Dorie left the room with Riley. "I'll go sit in the booth. I need a little distance from all this trauma."

Riley nodded and loped down the hallway to his office.

When he returned, Riley settled into his seat. "Recording on with Dr. Harrison, Mrs. Johnson, Felicity Johnson, Brian Griffith, and me, Captain Riley McDonough."

"Since Mrs. Johnson is unable to clearly remember that day and the accident, the District Attorney wants Mrs. Johnson in a long-term, secure memory care facility to be determined today as part of a plea deal. Ms. Felicity Johnson, if you agree to plead guilty for the burglaries, you will return any items you took from the churches and make restitution for any broken glass, door locks, etc. In addition, you will check in with a parole officer once a week until your one-year probation is complete. Are these terms acceptable?"

Dr. Harrison chimed in. "I for one am delighted with the care my patient with receive." He named a place in Atlanta. "I'll call it now to see if it still has an opening for Mrs. Johnson."

Riley indicated Dr. Harrison should stay seated. "I need to hear from Mrs. Johnson and Felicity Johnson. What do you say?"

"Yes, sir. I plead guilty to the break-ins and will return the things I took. I will reimburse the churches for the repairs they needed after I was there. One-year probation is fair."

"Mrs. Johnson, what say you?"

"I don't know. I didn't think I hit the boy. I'm so sorry."

The attorney piped up. "She can't plead guilty to something she doesn't remember."

"Then the DA has the right to require she check into a secure memory care facility to have her needs met daily. Dr. Harrison, I assume you approve."

At his nod, Riley stood. "Very well, Ms. Johnson, you have a week to comply with the return of the property and begin restitution. Ms. Johnson, Dr. Harrison, will you ride in the ambulance with Mrs. Johnson to help her get settled?"

At both nods, Riley stretched. "I declare us done. Ms. Johnson you are free to go with Mrs. Johnson."

Dorie settled herself in her SUV. She started the engine and asked the Bluetooth system to call Ross.

"Hello?"

"Ross, it's Dorie. I'm getting ready to leave the station. Where are you?"

"Signing paperwork on a new truck. Go on home. I can pick up something at Melody's Diner on my way home."

"By rights, that would be my job since I'll get home sooner."

"Darlin', you go home. You've been working all day. I've been playing and buying a truck. I'll pick up food. Change into something comfortable and play with the dog." He paused. "What's going to happen to Felicity?"

"The DA allowed her to go home on her own recognizance on one-year probation. Aunt Jac'line is being admitted to a secure long-term memory care facility for dementia and head trauma patients."

"Hey, I gotta go. The man with my keys just entered the room. Love ya."

The line went dead.

Dorie headed up the mountain to Helen.

Chapter 24
Is she, or isn't she?

When Dorie arrived home, she let the dog out and changed into her lounging pajamas. Then she set the table with their china and crystal from the wedding. In the center of the table, she placed a round plate with the pregnancy test box and covered it with their newest colander. Then she poured herself a Coke over ice, and, finally, felt ready and calm enough to call her mom.

When she answered, Dorie said, "Hi, Mom."

"Dorie, I've been so worried. Terry told me what happened. I've been trying to call, but you've not been answering your phone."

Tears ran down Dorie's face. She wiped them away with her napkin. "I know. I had to work through some things. I was angry at first. I wanted to be rational when we talked."

"Oh, Sweetheart, are you crying?"

"Even from St. Louis, you know who I am." Dorie wiped her face again. "I've met my two sisters. One of them was at the wedding as a server. Remember Jenny? With the light brown ponytail?"

"She and Riley seemed to hit it off, right?"

"Yes. I told you about Felicity. The lady Ross is partnering with at the ranger station is my sister as well."

"I knew, Dorie, it was a chance you'd run into family in Daelin. I wouldn't keep you from there if that was where God wanted you. When you met Ross, he was also a perfect fit for our family. He's my son just the same."

Dorie shared with her the history she'd learned and what had happened with her father, mother, and sisters.

"If I had known there were three of you, I would have adopted all of you. Your father may have been a little shocked, but we wanted a little girl. What's three?"

Dorie laughed. "Three girls with three boys? The Brady Bunch without an Alice the housekeeper. Can you just imagine the mayhem?"

"And the love, Dorie. It's all about the love. You needed someone to love you. We needed to love you. We knew as soon as we saw your beautiful auburn hair and dark brown eyes that you needed to come home with us. In fact, it was Terry that picked you out to begin with."

"Mom, there's one more thing." Dorie paused and stared at the colander. "I might be pregnant. I should know more later this evening."

Her mom shrieked with joy. "That's wonderful! Let us know when you know."

"I will, Mom. I think I just heard Ross drive into the garage. I better go."

"I love you, Dorie. Forgive us for forgetting you were someone else's little girl before you were ours."

"I love you too, Mom." Dorie hung up and wiped away the tears, the makeup, and the mascara. Then she jumped up to meet Ross at the door. Star also met her at the door as well.

"I'm finally home with food." Ross wrapped his arms around her and hugged her with the bags from Melody's. "You've been crying. Something wrong?"

"No, I just had a chat with Mom. Everything's back to normal."

He handed her the takeout bags, then he kissed her. "Let me go change into comfortable clothes too. Whoa! What's with the fancy dinner table? It's just burgers and fries, Babe. What's hiding under the colander? Dessert?"

Dorie laughed. "Not exactly. Just something I want to share with you tonight. Go change into something more comfortable."

Ross laughed. "We are eating, right? Not doing something else, are we? I'm kinda hungry."

"Yes, we're eating."

Ross bounded up the stairs with Star who was at his heels from the time he entered the house.

While Dorie plated the food, Ross and Star thudded on the floor above her. She smiled. It was perfect just the way it was. If they had a baby, it would be that much more perfect.

Ross finished every last French fry, including the ones on Dorie's plate. He even ate the rest of the hamburger she couldn't finish. "Is there dessert? Seriously?"

"We've got ice cream and cookies. Nothing out of the ordinary." Dorie grabbed his plate and used utensils. She stood and headed for the kitchen. "More coffee?"

"Of course. So, what's under the colander?" Ross called after her.

Dorie grinned. "Take it off and see. Just don't open it until I get back." She started soap and hot water in the sink to wash off the china and crystal.

Ross appeared behind her. She nearly dropped the china plate.

"Not what I expected. You don't know yet?"

Dorie rinsed the plates and put them in the drying rack. "Nope. I wanted us to know at the same time." She wiped her hands on the dish towel. "Go ahead. I've been dying to open it all day."

Ross opened the box flap and slid the test stick from the box. "Does this mean what I think it does?"

He held the test up where she could see it. A plus sign showed in the window.

"Yes. We're having a baby!"

Ross wrapped his arms around her. "I can't believe it. We didn't even know each other a year ago, yet we've met, married, and got pregnant in short order. I am so blessed. Are you okay with this, Dorie?"

"Surprisingly, yes. It's an honor to carry our child, Ross."

They kissed.

Chapter 25
Laying it all to rest …

The DNA results finally came back proving once and for all that Felicity, Jenny, and Dorie were indeed sisters.

When the third vehicle arrived in Oak Lawn Cemetery, the doors sprung open. Dorie and her two sisters emerged with bouquets of flowers, making it hard to hug each other. They walked together across the green grass, though it was early February. Ross and Riley climbed out, shook hands, and followed the ladies.

The breeze was cold. Dorie shivered. Ross caught up with her and wrapped an arm around her. She leaned into him.

Felicity called out to her. "Here it is." She indicated a double tombstone with the surname "Mackenzie." Beneath it were indicators for Paul and Selene and the dates of their births and deaths.

Jenny laid her bouquet of red roses between the graves. Felicity laid a bouquet of white roses on their father's grave. Dorie placed her bouquet of yellow roses on their mother's grave. They wrapped arms around each other.

"Lord God, You are the Creator of life. You are there at its inception and there at its end." Dorie paused. "These two people gave the three of us life through Your Hand. And You took them in Your love at their passing. Help us proudly represent them and You in our lives. Bless the new life growing inside two of us. Help us be together to help and love each other. Amen"

Felicity and Jenny repeated her Amen. Riley and Ross echoed them.

"I have albums of pictures at Aunt Jac'line's house. I didn't think to bring them. Why don't you come over for lunch?"

"That sounds like a great idea, Felicity." Dorie hugged her.

They walked back to the vehicles. Ross took Dorie's arm and offered an elbow to Felicity who took it. Jenny and Riley trailed behind them, deep in conversation.

"Are you coming for lunch, Jen?" Felicity hugged her.

Jenny looked at Riley. "I think Riley and I have some things to talk about. He'll bring me home later. I'll be over to see those photos soon."

Riley and Jenny drove to Java Joint.

"Espresso black for Riley. What can I get you, Jenny?" Angela called out to them as they came in the door.

Riley took her hand. "What do you want, Jenny?"

"Coke?" Jenny was usually the one serving guests.

"You got it. Take Dorie's booth unless you know she's coming."

"Dorie has her own booth?" Jenny whispered to Riley.

Riley laughed. "As a matter of fact, she does." He led her to the booth with the metal plate announcing it as Dorie's booth.

"They really do drink a lot of coffee." Jenny slid in on one side.

Riley slid in on the other. "Yes, though I suppose Dorie should cut down while she's pregnant."

"I can't believe I found my sisters, and they are each going to have a baby. It's unbelievable."

Jenny leaned back just as Angela slid the drinks onto the table.

"Anything else?" Angela never wrote anything down. Her memory was phenomenal.

Riley handed her a five to cover it. "I think we're fine. Just some privacy." Riley smiled at her and winked.

"You got it, Captain."

"You know everyone in town, don't you?" Jenny took a sip of her soda.

"We all grew up here and went to high school together. Now we're the ones running the businesses. The rest I've met in the course of my occupation. Didn't you go to Daelin High?"

"I changed schools almost every year until the Schaefers adopted me. We lived in Athens, Georgia, until their deaths. I moved to Aunt Flo's after that. By then I was a senior. I dropped out and took the

GED." Jenny gave him a hard look. "Don't beat around the bush, Riley. Go ahead and dump me. It will be okay."

Riley sat forward nearly touching her nose with his. "I don't want to dump you. I just want to talk."

"Dorie told me about your church rule about not dating non-Christians."

"Did she? That doesn't seem like Dorie." Riley sat back and crossed his arms.

Jenny leaned back too. "In point of fact, I asked her why it was so important to you that I go to church with you. She didn't mince any words."

"Oh, well, that does sound like Dorie." He uncrossed his arms. "The rule is not a church rule. It's a biblical, God one." Riley pulled his phone from his pocket. "I'll show you on my Bible app. See it's here, in 2nd Corinthians 6:14-16." He looked up to show her the passage into Jenny's stunned eyes. "What?"

"You literally have the Bible on speed dial on your phone?"

"Of course. This is the Bible Belt after all, Jen. Many people in the South put a lot of credence in the Bible. It can help to talk someone off a ledge or to give up a weapon. It's on my phone because it's handy." Riley couldn't believe she didn't understand the necessity of having the Bible available on the job. "It's better than trying to carry a book with me."

"How do you know what verses to use and where to find them?"

"Experience. I've been going to church and Sunday School since I was born. I became a Christian when I was eight. I don't know any other way to live life."

"I'm beginning to see what Dorie meant. Go ahead and show me the verse."

Riley read the text out loud. "Do not be yoked together with unbelievers. For what do righteousness and wickedness have in common? Or what fellowship can light have with darkness? What harmony is there between Christ and Belial? Or what does a believer have in common with an unbeliever? What agreement is there between the temple of God and idols? For we are the temple of the living God."

It was Jenny's turn to cross her arms. "So now I'm wicked and some kind of idol or devil? That's some pretty tough talk for someone who claims to be good."

"I'm not saying this well. Listen, if you yoke two oxen that aren't matched in strength and size, both of them are going to have a hard time plowing a field. Both will be chafed, and the job just won't be done well. That's all it's saying. If I marry someone who's not a Christian, we will always be at odds. We won't be trying to live the same kind of life." Riley shook his head. *How could he explain it?* "We wouldn't have the same goals in life."

"So, you are dumping me." Jenny began to slide out of the booth.

"Wait! I have a suggestion that might help us. I do think there could be an us. I'd really like there to be an us."

Jenny stopped and scooted back in. "What? I have to be a Christian though to make this relationship work, according to that verse."

Riley nodded. "But here's what I propose: Come

to church with me several times. See if God speaks to you. It won't help if I coerce you into 'getting saved.' You'll just resent me."

"This is really important to you, isn't it?" Jenny frowned. "I guess I can try it. Dorie and Ross seem really happy. Are they both Christians?"

"Yes. To both questions. To be honest, I'm jealous of what they have. I don't want to settle for less."

"Which is me right now?" Jenny sniffed and a tear ran down her cheek.

"It doesn't have to be that way, Jen."

Riley reached for her hands. She reluctantly surrendered them.

"I want this to work, but not if we're on opposite sides of this issue."

Jenny squeezed his hands. "I guess I can understand that. I'll give it a try and see what happens. I'm not going to do something just to keep you though."

"Nor do I want you to. Even if we don't become a permanent couple, I would still want you to be a Christian."

Jenny let go of his hands. "This really means a lot to you."

"It's what I believe. Jesus came to earth, fully God, fully man. He did miracles and taught God's truths to everyday people. He was crucified though He had no sin for the sins of the world. His blood takes the place of my sins, and God accepts me. Jesus was resurrected, alive after being mercilessly killed. One day God will welcome me into heaven as a result of Jesus' sacrifice. All I had to do was believe and ask for His forgiveness."

"Really? It sounds too easy."

Riley nodded. "Will you think about it?"

"This is in the Bible? Can you put that app on my phone?"

Riley took her phone and loaded the app. "Start reading in John." He bookmarked it for her. "Let me take you back home to Aunt Flo's now."

Dorie and Ross were working on dinner when a knock summoned them to the front door. Dorie ran to the door with Ross running behind her. They both arrived, giggling, and threw open the door.

"Hi." Riley laughed with them. "You guys are crazy."

Dorie hugged him. "How did it go with Jenny?"

"Not going to lie. I've had easier conversations." Riley shook hands with Ross. "I just needed to talk to you two. Do you realize how lucky you are?"

Dorie looked at her husband, tall, copper-bearded, with his strawberry blonde hair. He smiled. "Yes, blessed."

"Doubly blessed." Ross pulled her to him. "No, triple blessed with baby."

Riley sat on the stairs. "I love you guys. I told Jenny I'm jealous of you and your happiness. Is it wrong to want the same?"

Dorie sat down next to him. "No, Riley. God has someone for you. It may not be Jenny. Wait on your perfect one." Dorie slipped her arm around him.

"You've got to watch for her though. She might

throw coffee on you one Sunday morning." Ross smiled. "Stay for dinner, friend."

About the
Author

www.dianeetatumwriter.com
tatumlight@gmail.com

This book is Diane E. Tatum's thirteenth book
with Winged Publications and is also the fourth of
her Main Street Mysteries series. She began writing
in elementary school. Her first published book Gold
Earrings began as a short story in a high school
creative writing class. Diane taught middle school
for eleven years. She retired from teaching public
school when her husband told her to "come home
and write your stories" and bought her a laptop.
Diane writes her stories and is an adjunct professor

of English at the local community college. She is supported by her family: husband Ken, two sons and daughters-in-law, and four young grandsons. Diane's home in Tullahoma, Tennessee, includes a 20-year-old Jack Russell terrier and a 5-year-old retired racing greyhound.

See my Pinterest page for each of my books! Here's the link for *DNA Secrets*: https://www.pinterest.com/tatumlight/dna-secrets-book-4-of-main-street-mysteries/

Enjoy two bonus chapters! The first is from *Finding Love in the Fog of Aphasia* and the second is chapter 1 of Book 5 of Main Street Mysteries: *The Disappearing Diaspora*.

Discussion Questions for Book Club/Bible Study

1. DNA Secrets is the fourth book in this Main Street Mysteries series. What changes have you seen in the main characters as a result of their mystery adventures?

2. Dorie and Ross both take new jobs after their honeymoon in Scotland. How do these jobs use their strengths better than their old jobs? What challenges do they each face as a result?

3. Dorie is stunned to find out she's adopted. Do you know anyone who has been adopted? How did they feel when they found out?

4. Terry gets everyone ancestry-type genetic testing for Christmas. Have you done this type of DNA testing? What did you learn about yourself that you didn't know? Has anyone in your family traced your family tree? What are the pros and cons of participating in genetic testing?

5. Jeremiah 29:11 is cited in this story. How do you interpret that verse for you? How is it a comfort and a challenge?

6. Ephesians 1:4-14 tells that Christians are adopted into God's family. How does that mirror adoption of children on earth? Why is it a comfort and a challenge? How can this passage explain the plan of salvation to someone who's been adopted?

7. 2 Corinthians 6:14-16a advises Christians not to be in partnership with unbelievers. Why does it apply to more than just marriage? What are the pitfalls for Christians if they partner in marriage, business with a non-Christian?

8. Is Aunt Jac'line responsible for Todd Wilkins's death if she's not competent? Should Felicity bear responsibility for Aunt Jac'line's actions when she's at work? Why is this not a resolution for Todd's parents?

From *Finding Love in the Fog of Aphasia,*
where Ross MacAvoy makes a cameo appearance!
Chapter 10
A devil of a deal …

Noelle walked back to her office. She went to her desk and sat. Her favorite mug was on her desk full of coffee, with just the right cream and sugar she supposed by its caramel color. Celia's doing.

"Jamey, I need to tell you what has happened here today." She took a sip from the mug. Just right. "People are making deals that affect you without your input."

Jamey furrowed his brown eyebrows. "What?"

"Everyone wants me to be your speech pathologist. Your dad, Celia, Sullivan and Connor."

"Grandpa."

"Yes. If we take on a client relationship, we cannot date or appear to be dating."

Jamey frowned and shook his head. "No."

"There's more. Your dad believes that I can help you AND be the carrot at the end of the stick." Noelle took a deep sip to allow Jamey to process what she was trying to tell him.

"No!" He stood and ripped open her office door. He left, no doubt to catch his dad.

In a few moments, he was back.

"Explain." Jamey sat back down, but his leg was pumping with anger or anxiety, which she could only imagine.

"People say I'm the best speech pathologist for TBI. I don't know if that's true, but that's what your dad and grandpa have been told. Therefore, they want me to work a miracle to change you back into the prince and heir of their company." Noelle paused. "They know you want to date me, so they think we'll do our best work ever so that can occur."

"That's what … I thought … you … meant." His face was red, and his fist was clutching the arm of the chair. "No."

※ ※ ※

Jamey stormed from the building, at least as fast as a guy with a cane could. He climbed into the Spider and took off. He drove until he reached a ranger station near his favorite place on the Appalachian Trail in the Chattahoochee Forest. Even though the wind was powerful and cold, he was determined to reach the overlook he loved. The spot was a place where he found it easier to hear God speak to him without all the daily distractions and noise.

He zipped and buttoned his parka and wrapped a scarf around his hood to keep it up. He pulled his leather gloves from under the front seat and locked the car. Jamey headed up the Trail to the ridge where his special place was. He needed wisdom and guidance. Everyone wanted to make decisions for him. It was time he took back control of his own life, at least in so far as he could. Sure, there were still challenges to face down every day, but he wanted Noelle by his side to help him and love him, eventually, as his wife, not as merely a caregiver or speech pathologist.

He struggled on the incline to the overlook. It wasn't far from the ranger station or he wouldn't have attempted it. When he finally breached the top, he was hot and sweaty on this very cold day. He sat down on a fallen log after testing its security. Wouldn't have done that before the brain injury. He actually wouldn't have done many of the things he'd done in the last year, if not for the accident. He'd been a class A jerk. Now others were doing those things to him.

He bowed his head in prayer. If it would help, he'd pray out loud, but that would just be a struggle. God heard his innermost thoughts; that's what everyone said.

"God, help me. Heal me, not because I deserve it, but because only You are able. And give me a fighting chance with Noelle. She's the only one human who understands. I can't lose her. Fix this situation 'cause only You can. Change my dad and grandpa. Help me know what things to fight for and which things to submit to. Help me be the Christian I might have been if I'd been raised differently. I'm willing to be that person. Amen."

When Jamey opened his eyes, a large pair of hiking boots stood beside him. He looked up into the face of a tall and muscular forest ranger with red hair and a copper beard.

"You okay, sir?"

Jamey struggled to rise off the log. The ranger offered an arm, which Jamey gratefully accepted. "Yeah … praying."

"A church wouldn't be as cold, dude, but I totally get it. I'm closer to God here, too." The man laughed. "I'm Ross MacAvoy, your friendly neighborhood forest ranger. Can I help? It's a girl, isn't it? We guys always end up doing dumb things because of a girl. I just got married at Christmas, not that that was dumb."

Jamey smiled, then laughed. He handed him a card, which read, "I'm Jamey. I don't speak well due to Traumatic Brain Injury, but I understand what you say."

Ross gave him back the card and offered a handshake. "No problem, but why don't you come in for a cup of coffee? It's hot, which is more than I can say about yonder log."

Jamey nodded. "Yes."

"Now see there! You're talkin' a blue streak." Ross clapped him on the back and helped him back over the ridge, down the incline, and back to the ranger station.

When Ross opened the door for Jamey, heat escaped, inviting him in. He hadn't realized how cold he was until then. When he walked into the station, his phone began beeping with multiple texts.

"That would be your girl, I'd bet." Ross took off his parka and hung it on a peg in the wall behind his desk. "We've got a boosted Wi-Fi signal and 5G, in case of emergency."

Jamey pulled off his gloves and pulled his phone out of his pocket. He nodded. "No…Noelle."

"What do you like in your coffee?" Ross waited for his response.

"One teas … poon sugar. Cream."

"Come on back, and you can fix it yourself."

In the kitchen was a woman ranger with a long

blonde ponytail.

"Not getting any warmer out there, is it? I'm Felicity."

"Your … wife?" Jamey wondered what it would be like to work side by side with Noelle.

"Oh, no, no, no, no, no." Ross backed away like the kitchen was on fire. "Dorie'd have my hide if I even thought about letting you think that." He pulled his cellphone from his pocket. "This is my Dorie."

This girl in the photo was petite, had red-streaked hair cut in a short style, and a beautiful smile. It looked like the backdrop was Scotland. Dorie looked like she could be Felicity's sister, though.

"Looks … like … Scotland." Jamey felt the cold now that he was in the warm cabin. Even if he didn't have aphasia, he'd probably stutter anyway.

Felicity grabbed Jamey's arm. "No, don't get him started on the perfect honeymoon they had in Scotland. I don't think I can stand it. In fact, I could probably tell it by now." She laughed and walked back to the office area.

Ross roared with laughter. "Aye, it was perfect. I had the perfect wife to take with me. That's the secret. If your girl's perfect for you, don't let her get away."

"Good … advice." Jamey stirred his coffee and sat down at their kitchen table. "Okay … here?"

"Absolutely." Ross dragged a chair out and sat down with Jamey with his own cup of coffee. "Trust me when I say, you should answer those texts forthwith."

"That's the best piece of advice he's given you

yet!" Felicity's voice carried from the office.

Jamey laughed. "Not your … wife?"

"I know. Dorie calls her my work wife, but not in a good way, if you get my meanin'."

Jamey nodded and pulled out his phone. He scanned through the texts from Noelle, ignoring the ones from his dad and grandpa.

"Where are you?"

"Your dad is worried."

"You still need therapy, Jamey!"

"Answer. I'm getting worried now too."

"If you are hurt somewhere, your dad is going to sue me for malpractice."

"If what we might have is precious to you, you had better answer my texts."

The last one got his attention. He began calling her before he thought about his inability to speak in an emotional setting.

"Jamey, thank heavens! Are you okay? Where are you?" Noelle sounded upset.

"Mountains. … Praying." Jamey tried to stay calm, so his emotions didn't flood in on him, making it impossible to form words. "On the … ridge."

"Why didn't you answer me?" Tears, or the verge of tears, sounded in her voice.

"No … service." His brain began to flood. "In … ranger … cabin." He put his phone on speaker, so Ross could help him.

"Relax, Jamey. I don't want you to flood since you have to drive back." She paused. "Is someone with you?"

"Yes, ma'am. I'm a forest ranger here at the station, Ross MacAvoy. Jamey's just having a cup of coffee with me to warm up. He's perfectly fine. He says you're perfectly fine too."

Jamey hit the table. He could feel the blood surge into his face.

"Well, you did." Ross laughed. "He says you might be perfect."

"Well, that's not true, or I wouldn't be in the middle of this mess. Jamey, come down the mountain carefully. The wind is picking up. Let me know when you're in Daelin."

"You guys live in Daelin? I used to own the nursery that burned down. My wife used to work for the *Daelin Beacon*." Ross showed Jamey another picture on his phone of Dorie in her wedding dress.

"Didn't I read she was working with Daelin PD now?"

Noelle's voice sounded so far away. Jamey knew he couldn't lose her no matter whether he could speak or not.

"Yeah, I think she's safer working crime scenes than reporting on them." Ross poked Jamey. "You okay?"

Jamey grabbed the notepaper in the center of the table and a pencil and began writing.

"Noelle, Jamey's gears are turning, and he's writing something. Hang on a minute." Ross shot him a puzzled look.

"Read this … to her." Jamey handed the notepaper to him.

Ross furrowed his eyebrows. "Noelle, Jamey has a message for you. 'I'll talk to my dad and grandpa. I love you. Please wait for me, whatever happens.'"

"Oh, Jamey, I love you too. Come down off the mountain, and we'll figure this out together." No doubt remained that she was in tears now.

"Coming to you … soon. Finish … coffee." Jamey ached with having another man read his words of love to her, but how else would she know what was in his heart?

Chapter 1 of Book 5 Main Street Mysteries: *The Disappearing Diaspora*!

The creamy formal engraved invitation lay on the middle of the dining table. Dorie picked it up and read it again:

To: Ross MacAvoy +1

What: Daelin High School Reunion

When: June 4, 5, & 6

Where: Where else? Daelin High School

Why: To bring the scattered members of our high school back together for one weekend

RSVP by May 1. Details enclosed.

The pages enclosed detailed a flurry of events and activities, including a Friday night formal, a Saturday picnic with a pig roast, and a Sunday drinks and nibbles get-together at the Daelin Country Club.

Besides knowing few people who graduated from Daelin High School, Dorie was obviously pregnant by now and somewhat self-conscious of her growing abdomen. After all, she and Ross had only been married since Christmas, yet she was four months pregnant, a honeymoon conception. It was totally unexpected despite their resolve to have any children that God sent by avoiding the use of birth control. Being barely five foot, the baby had nowhere to go but outward.

"Ross, have you responded to this invitation? Angela is going to ask if we're coming when I go to Java Joint today."

Ross appeared at the top of the stairs, her ginger-haired giant of a man. "No, you've never agreed to go." He thudded down the stairs and wrapped her in his arms. "Do you want to go? I'm not going without you. You're the best thing that's happened to me in the last fifteen years. And our child, of course."

"Our child is obvious, Ross. I need to buy maternity clothes this weekend, or I'll have to stay home for the next five months in my nightgown."

"Now, there's an interesting proposition. Will you also be barefoot in my kitchen?" Ross placed his hand on her "baby bump." "You look beautiful, Darlin'. I'm proud to be your husband and the father of our child. Maybe you need some retail therapy. Buy something for the formal as well as some practical clothes. I'll call Angela from the forest today and let her know we're all in."

Dorie buttoned a button he'd missed when putting on his uniform. Ross was a ranger in the Chattahoochee forest along the Appalachian Trail. She hugged him close. "I so love you. I hate when you're gone two nights at the station."

"I know, Darlin'. Maybe one of your sisters could go shopping with you. Felicity probably knows a good maternity shop." Ross started coffee for them both in his fancy coffee maker. "Get stuff you want as well as need."

Dorie's oldest sister Felicity Johnson had been Ross's partner until recently. She was also pregnant, nearing six months now. The ranger service had fired her over her role in some burglaries that had occurred in Daelin, even though the charges had resulted in only a fine. The charges were still on her record. Her contract included a morality clause, which she broke by committing crimes and being pregnant outside of marriage.

Dorie tugged at her clothes, leggings and a gauzy tunic. *I may need to go find something more ... more... big.* As a petite, vivacious lady, her clothes were athletically styled with slim lines. In addition, she knew no one as small as she was to borrow from. Sigh. Shopping is immediately necessary.

Ross startled her with a kiss on her neck. "It's okay, Darlin'. You look lovely." He handed her decaf coffee in an insulated mug for the car. "I know it's not the same, but it's better for both you and the baby."

Dorie nodded and took a sip. "No, it's not the same. Thanks for the coffee and taking care of me. I guess I need to get going."

They kissed. Star, their rescued retired racing greyhound, snuggled into the space between them. Dorie laughed and headed for the door. She grabbed the cape they'd bought on their honeymoon in Scotland.

"Don't meet any bears today, ranger."

"Don't get into a jam with any criminals."

Dorie stepped out into the fresh spring mountain air. She took a deep breath. It tasted green with that metallic taint of early morning fog. She thought she felt a flutter of the child's movement.

"Well, good morning, little one."

Ross stepped out on the porch after her. "Beautiful mountain morning, my love."

"The baby moved." Dorie watched Ross's blue eyes grow wide. "I don't know when I'll feel him or her again, but he moved."

"Praise God!" Ross swooped her into his arms and hugged her tight. "It will be hard to top that. This is definitely the top of today's highlights."

They headed to their vehicles hand in hand. Ross started his new truck and headed up the mountain to the Chattahoochee. Dorie's SUV took her down the mountain road through Helen to the Daelin Police Department.

Dorie arrived just a few minutes before eight and piled her things into her Liaison Officer workspace. She booted the computer then hurried to the women's restroom, irritated at needing to frequent the facilities frequently.

When she exited the restroom, she ran into Chloe.

"Darn, Dorie, that baby is taking over, isn't it?" Chloe was the police lab technician.

"Thanks, Chloe. I'm already conspicuously pregnant, but I still have five months to go. Where is this child going to be?"

"Snuggled in your body, protected from the world. It's a good thing, friend." Chloe hugged her. "Lunch later?"

"I may need to go shopping instead of eating. My clothes don't fit." Dorie leaned back against the wall.

Chloe laughed. "Pretty sure you need to eat, too. Let me know, okay?"

Dorie nodded and went to her office. She was logging into the system when Police Captain Riley McDonough walked in and sat in the chair beside her desk.

"Dorie, you are glowing." Riley was Ross's best friend as well as her boss.

"Not you too! Everyone seems required to comment on my pregnancy today."

"It seems you just bloomed over the weekend. It's a good thing. Take the compliments and enjoy this time." Riley chuckled. "At least you know where your child is. Wait a few years. That will be a satisfaction."

"Do we have a case?" Dorie just wanted to change the subject away from her blooming self and her child.

"Yes. It's an odd thing. One of the reunion committee came into town to help Angela with the preparations. She's just disappeared." Riley shook his head. "Lucy Hendrickson was my first crush back in high school." He handed her the file. "See if there's any insight you can give to the case. Talk to Angela."

Ross walked into the ranger station cabin. His newbie sat at Felicity's old desk. He missed her already. She'd been prickly, but familiar, like Dorie.

"You must be Caleb Bryant." Ross stuck out his hand. "I'm Ross MacAvoy."

"I remember you from high school. Always taller than most folks in the hallway." Caleb shook Ross's hand heartily. "Going to the reunion?"

"Yes, I need to call Angela this morning. I've been waiting for my wife to weigh in. She grew up in St. Louis." No need to go into all the details with a stranger about her sisters being here.

"So, you're married?"

"Yes and expecting a child." Ross checked the computer screen for hikers in the area. "What about you?"

"No, haven't found the right girl." Caleb seemed to mean more than he said. "I'm hoping some of them decide I turned out okay and might want to take a chance on me."

Ross was picking up a strange vibe from Caleb. If he'd been Spiderman, he'd say his spider sense was tingling. Instead, Caleb just seemed … creepy.

"Let me show you around while it's quiet." Ross stood up and motioned for him to come with him. "Now that it's getting warmer, and weather in general is better, we'll get some day hikers on the trail, mountain bikers too. First duty of everyday: whoever gets here first makes the coffee."

Ross gave commentary while he filled the big urn with water and coffee. "Notice the "Where are YOU?" board. Whenever you leave the station, you need to indicate where you are so we can keep each other safe. I'll talk about the other safety measures we have in place to keep rangers safe, protocols to keep hikers safe, and the refrigerator keeps our food safe."

Ross started the coffee and leaned against the countertop. "We get mail for hikers. We have a scheduler online to keep track of hikers. We also care for wildlife and natural environment around the area."

"That seems like a lot to keep track of." Caleb crossed his arms and furrowed his brow. "And we sleep here two nights in three."

"No rest for the weary. There's a bunk room for

your stuff." Ross pointed out Caleb's duffel. "Coffee will be ready soon. Stow your things. Come back with questions."

Caleb grabbed his belongings and put them in the bunkroom.

Ross just prayed the coffee would be ready soon.